CHRONICLES OF A TIMEBOUND WARRIOR

L. S. WESTHOFF

Medieval Earth Realm

"No matter the chains, no matter the pain, I will never betray the fire in my soul."

ISBN 978-1-964165-93-6

Disclaimer

This novel contains mature content, including depictions of violence and gore, explicit sexual scenes, and descriptions of torture. These elements are part of the fictional narrative and are intended to contribute to developing of the story and its characters. While these scenes do not dominate the plot, they are present and may be distressing to some readers. Reader discretion is advised. If you are sensitive to these themes, please consider this disclaimer carefully before proceeding. This novel draws inspiration from historical events, names, and places.

Contents

ONE

Justice Served

A storm is brewing in the ancient kingdom of Eldoria, where towering trees whisper secrets and rivers sing songs of forgotten times. As the sun dips below the horizon, its warm light casts everything around me in a golden glow. But the brightness of the day can't chase away the darkness weighing on my heart.

I'm ready, every fiber of my being focused on one purpose: to confront the opposition in the circular sparring ring. A small crowd of warriors has gathered, their whispers of anticipation filling the air. They're all eager to witness the duel that will decide the fate of two kin—myself and my uncle, Galadron. I grip Ashbringer tightly, feeling its powerful energy pulse through my hand. Today, justice will be served, and the truth of Galadron's cruelty will be exposed.

I walk slowly toward the sparring ring, lost in thought. The soft glow of the late afternoon shadows goes unnoticed as I struggle to control my anger. My emerald eyes narrow as they lock onto Galadron, who stands ready in the sparring ring. I don't take my eyes off him for a moment.

Stepping into the ring, I see Galadron sneer as he readies his sword. With a nod from the overseer, the battle begins.

I waste no time, moving with lightning-fast Elven speed to deliver the first strike. Galadron, not one to be outdone, blocks my blow with equal precision. Our swords clash with a thunderous sound, sending a shower of sparks into the air. I quickly sidestep and unleash Ashbringer's blazing heat as it slices through the air. He barely manages to deflect the attack, his arms trembling under the force.

Galadron's Elven abilities allow him to evade my next strike, countering with short and fast blows that force me to retreat. But my determination is unyielding, and I press on. We dance with death, our movements blurring with speed and skill, each of us seeking an opening. A fierce grin curls my lips as I unleash a barrage of strikes, my eyes scanning for any weakness in his defenses.

Galadron parries my strikes, but I can see him beginning to weaken as the fight wears on. Suddenly, I spot my opening. I duck as his sword slices through the air above my head and hurl Ashbringer toward him. The sword leaps from my grip, slicing through his defenses and leaving a trail of smoke and blood in its wake.

Ashbringer quickly returns to my hand, ready for the next attack. Galadron staggers backward, his breath coming in ragged gasps. He switches his sword to his off-hand, his dominant arm now useless. I advance aggressively, my eyes locked on him. With a final decisive strike, I send him to his knees, his sword flying through the air and landing in the dirt.

"Galadron, you stand accused of unspeakable cruelty and tarnishing our kinship with the vilest acts. I challenged you, and you accepted a duel to the death."

He raises his gaze to me, showing no remorse, only defiance. "What I have done with the animals is of no concern to you," he spits, his words dripping with hate. "They are just tools to me, nothing more." He leans over, coughing up blood, and spits onto my boots.

My grip tightens around the hilt of my sword, my knuckles turning white. I am furious at myself for trusting this monster with my beloved horses. I missed the senseless abuse he inflicted. Placing the tip of Ashbringer under his chin, I force him to look into my eyes, then swiftly cut off his head.

I bend down and wipe my sword on Galadron's lifeless body. With each stroke, I remove the remnants of our confrontation in a silent ritual of closure. I step over his lifeless form and slowly walk away, my movements deliberate and heavy with emotion. The weight of my actions hangs in the air as I leave the scene behind. Despite the difficulty of the moment, I remain resolute and determined to face whatever consequences may follow.

***

As I walk away from the ring, the crowd parts in silence, their eyes following my every move. From the shadows, a figure emerges, his silver hair glinting in the fading light. It is Renalt, Captain of the Guard and my mentor, who has been away on a diplomatic mission. He approaches the ring, his expression unreadable.

"Anwen," Renalt calls softly, his voice carrying the weight of unspoken questions. "What has happened here?"

I pause, turning to face my mentor. "Galadron has paid for his crimes. He abused my horses and treated them with extreme cruelty. I couldn't let it go unpunished," I reply, my voice steady but laced with lingering anger.

Renalt's eyes harden as he looks at Galadron's lifeless body. "Justice is served, then," he says quietly. "But now I fear your father's reaction to all of this."

I furrow my brow in concern. "What do you mean?"

"He won't take it easy on this act of defiance by dueling a kinsman without permission."

I don't care about the consequences. "Serious actions require intense repercussions. He agreed to the duel. I do not regret taking his life."

Renalt's brows furrow with concern. "Anwen, your father—"

"I don't care about the consequences," I cut him off, my tone firm. "He had it coming."

Renalt sighs, realizing my determination.

"Would my father care about his precious reputation with the Council of Elders if a man had challenged a duel to the death? No, he would explain it away. Father wants to control my every action. He should know better by now."

Neither of us notices as a stealthy courier slips away from the castle to inform Lord Roderick Elwen of what happened today.

***

The next day, my father, Lord Elwen, sits in the chamber of the Council of Elders. His brow is furrowed with concern, and his fists are clenched tightly on his lap. The council members murmur amongst themselves, their voices humming low in the dimly lit room.

A stern-faced man with a long white beard, one of the elders, clears his throat and addresses my father. "Your daughter's actions have caused quite a stir, my lord," he says, his tone dripping with disapproval. "Challenging her uncle to a duel to the death is unprecedented for our females, even for one as headstrong as Anwen."

"This horrific incident has threatened the whole social structure of Eldoria! This must not happen here," another elder chimes in. "Punish Anwen for her acts toward an Elven kinsman, my lord!" they chant in unison.

My father's jaw tightens as he meets the elder's gaze. "I am well aware of my daughter's actions, Elder Thalion," he replies, his voice barely concealing his frustration. "And rest assured, she will face the consequences of her recklessness. But for now, we must focus on the matter at hand."

The elder nods gravely, but his eyes betray a hint of skepticism. "Indeed, my lord. But let us not forget the delicate balance we must maintain within our kingdom. Anwen's actions could have far-reaching consequences."

My father's expression darkens as his thoughts race, contemplating the ramifications of my impulsive behavior. As the council deliberates behind closed doors, the fate of House Elwen hangs in the balance, and its future is uncertain in the wake of my defiance.

The Council's decision is given to my father. Elder Thalion says, "The Council agrees that Anwen needs to be controlled. She is to be married immediately, and her husband will be held responsible for her behavior."

My father nods in understanding. "I will abide by the Council's decree."

Meanwhile, back at the sparring ring, Renalt and I are honing our hand-to-hand combat skills. Little do we know that a storm is brewing on the horizon, threatening not only our family but the very foundation of Eldoria itself.

My victory may be seen as justified in defending my family's honor and seeking justice for the cruelty inflicted upon our horses. However, the legality and morality of my actions are subject to interpretation, especially in the eyes of my father, Lord Elwen, and the Council of Elders.

As the sun sets over the ancient kingdom, casting long shadows across the land, the echoes of my challenge reverberate through the trees, heralding the dawn of a new era filled with uncertainty and strife. My fate hangs in the balance, and only time will tell whether my victory in the duel will be overshadowed by the consequences of my actions.

TWO

Merging of Houses

The new day starts bright and clear. The early sunlight comes in through the main hall windows where I am sitting alone and breaking my fast. After the duel and the fallout that is to happen, I can't find peace. I am interrupted by my father's loud steps as he walks into the room, his presence casting a big shadow over the peaceful morning. He has returned from his duties with the Council of Elders.

I look up from my food. My face is as calm as before, but I can feel the heat in my father's eyes. I see his angry expression, showing his strong emotions. Without any greetings, he starts to take his anger out on me due to the circumstances I have created after killing my uncle in the duel. His words pour out like a waterfall of shock and disbelief.

"Do you even understand the situation? You have created chaos in Eldoria!" My father says angrily. "How could you challenge your uncle to a duel to the death without informing me?"

I stare at him with no fear.

"He was a monster. That's why I put him down. I don't need your permission or anyone else's." I interject, my voice cutting through the tension like a blade.

I look straight ahead, not backing down under my father's hard stare. But my boldness only makes him angrier. He keeps criticizing my actions, his voice getting louder with each blaming word. I listen without reacting and grow tired of his rambling on.

Finally, when my father's angry speech reached its highest point, I got up smoothly from my seat, moving with purpose as I prepared to leave the main hall. I give my father a long look and a silent dare in my eyes before I walk confidently out of the castle toward the stable.

The air is fresh and energizing outside, a nice break from the stuffy inside of the castle walls. I head toward the stables, my footsteps echoing off the stone path as I easily move through the familiar area.

As I get closer to my destination, I see someone coming from the corner of my eye. It's Sarbalar Molil, a representative from House Loradar, and I am not in the mood for his attempts at manipulating me.

I make a face as I watch him come closer. I dislike that man, and anyone could clearly see that in my expression. I know that my father and Sarbalar have been discussing expanding their relationship into a partnership that could help both houses. But I am not interested in such partnerships; I have my own way to go.

With a tired sigh, I pull out my reliable sword, Ashbringer, and tell it to light up. The sword catches fire at my thought, its bright light shining against the dark background of the stables.

Sarbalar hesitates to get any closer to me, for everyone knows how dangerous my sword's enchanted abilities are. He starts to lose confidence when he sees how determined I am. But I don't go easy on him. I hold my sword, Ashbringer, firmly and start to swing it in a controlled way. This is my silent way of warning Sarbalar to stay away.

"Not this again; I need to talk to you, Anwen. Put your weapon away," he grumbles, sounding frustrated.

But I don't budge, for I am not affected by Sarbalar's weak attempts to convince me.

Oh, I love being told what and when to do something. "That's not going to happen, Sar. I have things to do," I reply, my voice determined.

"I am here because your father wants to discuss dates for our immediate union." He gives up with a sigh of disappointment and leaves, his footsteps echoing on the stone path that leads him back to the castle.

As Sarbalar's footsteps become quieter, I sigh tiredly and feel the burden of my duties. But I know that I have to make my own way and won't let others influence me. I turn with a determined walk back toward the stables, already thinking about the challenges I'll face next.

I know I am the only one who will inherit House Elwen, and damn if I will let a man-child control me and my property. It's time to start looking for ways out of this situation.

As I stride toward the stables, the weight of responsibility is heavy on my shoulders. I see Finn, my loyal companion, engaging in a playful interaction with a mare. Even though I am deep in thought, I can't help but smile as I watch the big, beautiful horse. He is a massive 17-hand black warhorse, happily enjoying himself.

Finn sees me and stomps his front hoof in frustration.

"Come on, old man. Let's stretch those legs on a good run to the forest," I mind-speak with Finn, amusement lacing my voice.

Finn snorts in response, eager to be released from the confines of the stable. We both enjoy a good run.

I easily put the saddle and bridle on Finn, something we are as used to as the rhythm of our own hearts. As I mount up, I feel Finn's powerful muscles bunch and flex with the excitement of a run. Finn prances and pulls at the bit to go, straining to leap forward, and I laugh at his impatience.

But how can the journey be complete without my faithful companion, Maynard, the hawk whose keen eyes and swift wings have accompanied me on countless adventures? I call her forth with a sharp whistle, and she descends from the sky in a graceful swoop, landing lightly on my shoulder.

"We're going for a run, Maynard." I mind-speak, my inner voice barely above a whisper. The hawk squeezes my shoulder and lifts off in flight.

I lean to whisper into Finn's ear, "Let's do this." Finn leaps forward and charges out of the stable. His strong muscles push us with great force and speed. The sound of his hooves hitting the ground is steady and reliable, like a heartbeat, as we rush toward the far-off forest, a peaceful place in a chaotic world.

Right now, I feel the excitement of going fast, the joy of riding, and the strong connection between Finn and me. I get lost in the rhythm of Finn's steps and the wind in my hair, and for a brief moment, everything feels perfect.

But as the sun starts to set, casting long shadows on the ground, I start to feel a sense of dread. Far away, I see a dark cloud on the horizon, a sign of the coming storm.

I hear Maynard call out and look up at her, smiling and feeling lighter and free.

And in an instant, that changes...

THREE

The Mysterious Portals

Finn runs a good mile or so, and we enter Dawnsong, the enchanted forest. Despite years spent in and around it, I've never quite understood how this forest earns its rapture. Today seems no different; everything appears ordinary. I slow Finn down as we approach the river running through the forest. I dismount to let him drink from the freshwater stream and relax as the sun warms my face.

Suddenly, a strange sensation washes over me as if a strange force is passing through my body, aligning my cells in an unfamiliar way. Finn's unease becomes evident as he gazes at the sky anxiously and senses something weird. Maynard reacts with distress, her claws digging into my shoulder in a desperate attempt to anchor herself. The air around us feels charged and almost electric as if reality is shifting or something is unsettling.

"By the gods, do you feel anything strange?" I barely have time to say before a swirling portal opens, and we are violently yanked through it.

On arrival, Finn sees that I am bleeding profusely from a cut artery in my arm and am unconscious. Finn has a few cuts to his legs that are already healing. Maynard tells Finn she has no injuries but just a few lost feathers.

Finn feels weakened but manages to shift to his dragon form and carefully approaches me. Finn knows that his dragon blood has healing abilities. His talon opens his finger and he drops blood into my wound. The wound bleeding slows then stops and the skin edges start to pull together and heal.

I open my eyes and slowly try to get my bearings, blinking away the last bits of memory. My head feels fuzzy, like after a long sleep. I'm sprawled on the cold, damp ground by the riverbank, and the smell of wet grass and rushing water fills my nose. My elbows dig into the sand as I push myself up, and a wince escapes my lips from the dull ache in my head.

Finn's worried gaze meets mine instantly. He scans me from head to toe to check if I've got any injuries. A rustle in the nearby branches draws my attention to Maynard. She perched on a sturdy limb, and her sharp eyes locked on me. A low chirp escapes her beak as a question hangs in the air.

I checked on my friends quickly, and I was relieved. They appeared shaken but thankfully unharmed. My heart's frantic rhythm, which pounded against my ribs, began to slow.

"Finn, what happened?" I ask, slowly getting to my feet. A slight grogginess and tiredness linger.

"I'm not sure, but you were injured," Finn explains, his voice steady. *"I used my blood to heal you."*

I look around carefully, taking in everything. This place feels totally different from our forest by the river. The smells are strange, and the plants look different, unlike any I've seen before in the forest.

Then I remember the strange and swirling doorway we came through—the portal. It must have taken a ton of magic to create something like that. But the portal is gone and vanished without a trace, and an easy way to return to our own world has gone with it.

"We're not in Eldoria anymore," I say, the reality sinking in.

I see blood on my arm and the ground, which is a firm reminder of the chaos that has immersed us. Finn's concerned eyes meet mine, reflecting my own confusion.

"Finn, are you able to travel? I asked, *"Maynard, can you scout the area?"*

They both nod, their faces grim. Finn stretches, his body glowing for a moment before transforming back into his massive warhorse form. I swing myself onto his back, feeling the familiar comfort of the saddle. Maynard takes flight with a powerful flap of her wings, soaring high above the trees to get a better look at what lies ahead.

Finn and I start walking together and splash carefully through the shallow part of the river. We're now officially in this strange forest; everything seems so different from what we know. The towering trees cast strange shadows on the ground, and the leaves whisper in a language I don't understand. My brain feels fuzzy while I'm trying to piece together what just happened and how we ended up in this weird place.

Maynard returns and shares her observation. *"Nothing looks familiar. There is a castle that lies about two to three miles southwest."*

"Then we head in that direction," I tell them, urging Finn forward. *"Let's find out where we are and who brought us here."*

As we continue, the forest grows denser, and the trees tower above us like ancient protectors. My heart hammered in my chest as we emerged from the trees. The air is thick with the scent of unfamiliar flowers, and the sounds of strange creatures echo through the woods. Each step takes us further into the unknown, but with Finn and Maynard by my side, I feel more in control than before.

I'm still at a loss trying to make sense of the situation.

About a mile into our journey, I hear male voices and horses walking through the forest in our direction. I tell Maynard to observe from the sky and pull up Finn to remain hidden behind a few trees. From our vantage point, we can see into an open area and watch two warriors on warhorses walking into the clearing.

The men are imposing, large, and muscular. They wear knight's silver armor, and both ride large warhorses. Black and grey symbols on their chests mark them as crucial fighters. One male in particular stands out. He has dark hair, a scruffy beard, and a deep voice. He handles his mount expertly. I recognize him as a fellow warrior and leader. I am intrigued; he has caught my eye and interest. Many elven males have attempted to catch my eye, but none piqued my interest. This male rides in, and I can't stop watching him.

Dark hair's warhorse stops, raises his head, and looks in our direction.

Finn says, *"We've been spotted."*

I roll my eyes and give him a snarky reply, *"You think?"* I urge Finn forward into the clearing; I might as well get this over with. I glamour my pointed ears to become rounded, like the human ears.

As we approach, Dark hair eyes me suspiciously, scanning me for weapons and for any other warriors behind me. Clever boy, he is checking all angles for a possible attack. His wingman remains silent.

Time to play the damsel in distress. "Good day to you; nice day for a ride, huh?"

Dark hair remains suspicious and doesn't respond.

Well, this is awkward. Finn is laughing way too loud and long in my head about this situation.

Dark hair tilts his head and squints his eyes as he looks at Finn's head, then shifts his gaze to me. He looks up at my right shoulder—exactly where Ashbringer's handle is located. That is strange, for Ashbringer is cloaked and invisible across my back.

Annoyed, I quip, "Well, can either of you talk or should we try to communicate in grunt language?"

Dark hair snaps his eyes back to mine, and oh, those eyes are a stunning blue-green. He says, "Are you alone, or are there others?"

"Alone and in need of shelter for a few days. Any suggestions?" He seems to be sizing us up and making his decision.

"I can offer you shelter for a few days. My castle is a short ride from here. First, I need your name and house."

"Of course, I am Anwen Elwen of House Elwen. I wanted to take a long ride and became lost."

"I am not familiar with your house. My name is Ashton Everest, of House Lionsway."

I nod my head at Ashton, and Finn is shouting in my head, *"Take him up on the offer; I'm starving."* I hide my smile.

"Thank you, Ashton, for your kind offer; I accept."

Ashton says nothing as they turn their mounts to lead the way to our next destination.

I signal for Maynard to follow discreetly as we set off with Ashton toward his castle, curiosity and caution swirling in my mind about this unexpected turn of events.

Time will tell if this is a mistake.

FOUR

Ride to the Forest

We keep riding behind Ashton, and my mind buzzes with questions about his true identity. His commanding presence suggests leadership far beyond that of a typical knight. As I study his powerful form, an unexpected attraction stirs within me. He suddenly turns in the saddle while sensing my gaze, catches my eye, and gives me a little side-smirk smile before turning back. And that smirk – there's something about it that I find annoyingly charming.

We continued to ride in silence for miles. The journey was quiet, with only the sound of our horses' hooves, the creaking of our leather saddles, and the rustling of leaves breaking the silence. I watched our surroundings, noticing how the forest changed as we moved deeper into Ashton's territory.

Finally, the castle comes into view. Interestingly, the gates are closed, and his castle is in defensive mode. The castle gates are imposing and have iron twisted into complex patterns. We are met by towering stone walls adorned with banners displaying the House

Lionsway symbol—a lion in silver and black. Armored guards watch us closely, recognizing their lord and his unexpected guests. As we come near the gates, they creak open and expose a courtyard flowing with activity. Ashton gives the guards quick instructions before leading us through the gates into the castle's courtyard.

The people within the castle walls are dressed in a strangely elegant style, moving with caution as they notice our arrival. Their expressions reveal they're clearly curious about us, but there's also a hint of wariness in their eyes.

We enter the castle courtyard and dismount at the barn enclosure. The stable boys offer to take Finn, but I decline. Finn does not want others to care for him. Ashton is watching and tells the stable boys to abide by my wishes.

I bring Finn to an open stall with a paddock, remove his gear, and ensure he is provided with fresh water, hay, and cracked oats. When Finn is in horse form, he does everything a horse would but must shapeshift occasionally. He tells me he is fine for now and wants some downtime, and he noted a beautiful dappled grey mare upon entering the barn he wants to get to know. I boop his nose, and we laugh, knowing he is content and that I can leave him without worrying.

I checked on Maynard; she has found a dry, quiet place to roost for the evening.

Walking out of the barn, I see Ashton waiting for me. Strange, but it's kind of him to do this personally.

He says, "I want to welcome you properly to my home and show you to your accommodations. We will have a meal served in approximately an hour. I took the liberty of having a bath drawn for you and additional clothing provided."

A mysterious aura surrounds Ashton – an intuition beyond a mere knight. My internal struggle intensified, especially as Ashton's actions seemed to peel away layers, revealing a complexity I couldn't dismiss.

I hate to admit it, but I've got to award points to Ashton. I follow him again, watching those flexing backside muscles and broad shoulders as we walk toward the castle. He is tall and has to be strong to be able to wear his heavy armor and wield his weapon effectively.

Inside the castle, there is a blend of old-world grandeur and practical living. Servants hurry about preparing for our arrival while knights and other residents move purposefully through the corridors. Ashton gracefully walks through the hall and asks for me to follow him deeper into the castle.

We walk through halls lined with stories of heroic tales and ancient battles, each telling an anecdote of bravery and honor. His home feels like a living history book, where every stone holds the memories of his family's past struggles and pride.

We ascend the stairs to what is to be my room. He stops at the door near the stairs and takes my hand, gently kissing it with those sensually full, warm lips. He lets go of my hand and says he will retrieve me for dinner. I thank him and enter my room; my thoughts are chaotic and erotic. My face is flushed, and I need that bath to cool it off.

The room is spacious and well-appointed, with a large four-poster bed draped in rich fabrics. The bath is already drawn and steams invitingly. I strip off my travel-worn clothing and armor and sink into the deliciously hot water, feeling the tension melt away. I wash my hair and sit for a few minutes, savoring the relaxation. My thoughts wander back to Ashton. There's something undeniably intriguing about him, something that stirs emotions *that* I'm not sure I'm ready to face.

After the bath, I check the clothing in the closet and admire the beautiful dresses. Although I prefer practical attire, I can tolerate a dress for a short time. I pick a crème and green embroidered dress with small cap sleeves and matching satin green shoes. Everything is about one size too large but manageable.

A female chambermaid knocks at the door who is sent to do my hair and attend to anything else I might need. I am already feeling drowsy and nearly fall asleep as she combs out the knots and deftly twists my long brown hair into an intricate design atop my head. It's been a long day, but the prospect of hot food makes me ravenous.

Another knock at the door is Ashton. I now understand the term "smoldering eyes" as his gaze travels from my head to my toes. Feeling weirdly shy and out of place, I take his extended arm, and we proceed downstairs to the evening meal.

He escorts me to a chair beside his, and we settle in for a meal. I steal a moment to look him over. Dressed in all black, the tight material highlights his impressive physique. The word that comes to mind is "delicious."

Maybe I am attracted because he is so different from elven men. Elf men are fair-colored, lithely muscular, and tall, but their features are more refined. Ashton is the opposite: dark coloring with physical characteristics that are rugged and tough in nature.

A mysterious aura surrounds Dark Hair—an intuition beyond a mere knight. My internal struggle intensifies, especially as his actions reveal a complexity I can't dismiss.

I mentally scold myself. He is not mine. I need to stop ogling him and focus on finding a way back home. My friends and your kingdom depend on you.

Ashton helps put various foods on my plate, proving himself an excellent host. I am barely awake, my full belly and tired body weighing me down.

Dark Hair begins his interrogation by seizing the moment.

"I noted your armor is of royal origins. You are not from this area and have a slight accent, which I have yet to place. Where are you really from, Anwen? Why were you alone and unprotected in my forest today? Are you married or perhaps betrothed?" He doesn't pause long enough for me to answer, and I start dozing off.

A touch on my arm jolts me awake to his gentle chuckle.

"I don't think I have ever had a woman fall asleep on me during a conversation or other things."

My face burns with embarrassment, and I quickly ask to be excused due to fatigue. He agreed and stood to help me get back to my room, but I refused his offer. I need to be away from this situation. I am just too tired to engage in more banter.

As I climb the stairs, I can feel his eyes on me. While reaching my room door, I entered only to find I had stepped into the wrong room. Ashton's sidekick is engaged in a lively encounter with a chambermaid, and she enjoys his attention. He looks over at me, smiles, and never stops, causing my face to flush hot again. I quickly back out, shutting the door, and try to figure out where my room is. Will this day never end?

I open another door, hoping it's my room, and enter. It is dark, and at this point, I don't care. I find the bed, climb in with my clothes on, kick off my shoes, and wrap the bedspread around me, falling into a deep and fast sleep.

I dream of a dark-haired and blue-green-eyed man whispering to me. I can't understand what he's saying, but he gently removes my gown. His large, warm hands skim across my shoulders and arms, lightly brushing my nipples. They instantly peak, and I start to move my hips, wanting something more. His finger traces the contours of my ear, and I moan, for elf ears are extremely sensitive.

A deep voice softly chuckles and whispers, "Not yet, little one, but soon you will be mine." I sigh, feeling the covers wrapped around me, and drift back to sleep in a dreamless, safe place.

I woke the next morning to soft sun rays streaming across my bed. I'm in my chemise with my dress draped over a chair and shoes next to it.

I don't remember getting undressed. I vaguely remember a delightful, naughty dream, but I'm still sleepy.

I decide to work that out after I've broken my fast. I choose not to wear a dress and opt for my armor instead. Now, I feel like I am in control again.

I head downstairs and find the main indoor kitchen. The head cook nods to me as I enter. She has kind eyes and a rounded figure that speaks well for her food. She easily smiles at me and asks what I would like to eat. I ask for bread, butter, and bacon, and she quickly assembles my meal. I thanked her and sat at the small table to eat my meal.

She introduces herself as Stella and says she knows I am important to Ashton. I laugh; every castle has lightning-fast gossip. She asks me what my favorite food is, and I quickly respond: cookies, any kind. She laughs and says she will have some made just for me. I smile and decide I like Stella. I excuse myself to check on Finn and find out where Maynard is holed up.

I enter the barn to check Finn's stall and paddock. He isn't there. Panic sets in—who would have messed with him and moved him? I mind-speak with Finn, and he immediately responds that he is in the pasture. I get directions to the back-pasture area and walk out to find him. As I come around a clump of trees, I hear Finn tell me to give him a few moments. Too late. I walk in on Finn and that little dappled gray mare going at it. Dang it—everyone around here seems to be busy with someone!

Finn laughs and assures me he'll be done in a bit. I excuse myself and hightail it out of there, calling for Maynard. She responds to my call and flies to my extended hand. We nuzzle each other, and she fills me in on what she's discovered.

Maynard describes the layout of the castle's exterior and surrounding areas. She promises to continue updating me with her findings.

"Don't look for Finn right now; he's busy." she says with a chuckle before taking flight.

Yep, he's certainly busy.

As I leave the pasture, Ashton standing in the central yard, arms crossed and watching me. Can a girl not catch a break? I tramp past him, searching for the warriors' sparring area.

I am unable to find it, so I reluctantly ask, "Hey, Dark Hair, where do you hide your warrior sparring area?"

He swivels his head toward me while narrowing his eyes. "Use my first name, and I'll take you there. Maybe even give us both a workout."

Oh, I would love that.

"Okay, Ash-ton, let's go." He rolls his eyes and starts walking to the sparring area.

Only two warriors are sparring now. Ashton says something I can't hear to them, and they leave as I warm up.

I ask, "Don't want your warriors to see you losing the sparring match to a woman?" I call Ashbringer, and he materializes in my right hand.

Ashton smirks. "No, little one. I don't want you to be embarrassed when I take you down."

Oh, he is a cocky one; this is going to be fun.

He starts to warm up, swinging his large sword in long and sweeping movements that showcase his power and control. Impressive. I'll need to be careful with this one.

"I see your sword is of fine craftsmanship. Elven origin, correct?" Ashton asks, eyeing Ashbringer.

"Yes," I reply, intrigued.

"I'm surprised a human knows anything about Elven." He shouldn't know about Elven people. He's more unusual than I thought.

Ashton says, "My mother was Elven, my father was human."

Elven and human relationships and their offspring are not allowed in Eldoria. He could be in danger for his life if the Court of Elders in Eldoria knew this. I have never met anyone from both races, and I wonder what magic or skills he possesses.

We enter the round sparring area, acknowledge each other, and I suggest three points to win; he agrees, and the competition is on. I don't like to lose. I measure him by a few feet, noting his tells; I can't judge his speed yet, so here we go. I am a blur of speed, weapon at my side, and as he goes into his defensive stance. I leap over his head and tap the middle of his back. He swings around quickly, a startled look on his face, and I laugh – had this been true combat, I would have split his spine into two pieces.

I tilt my head to the side and say, "One point for me, come on big boy, let's see what you've got."

The next thing I know, he is standing in front of me with his sword pointing at my throat. Never has any male bested me in sparring, and I am shocked.

Ashton says, "You surprised me with your speed and agility, but I know a few tricks of my own. One point for me, little one."

"I am not your little one." I backflip and tell Ashbringer, "Tap his right hamstring now."

Ashbringer immediately materializes behind Ashton, taps his hamstring, and instantly returns to my right hand.

"Well, now your hamstring would be cut, and your main fighting leg would be useless, so one point for me," I say while smiling, genuinely enjoying our sparring.

In a shimmer of movement, Ashton appears behind me and pulls me against his front.

He whispers in my ear, "You are an admirable fighter, but you still have more to learn. I can teach you many things you will enjoy."

His words arouse and infuriate me at the same time. As I turn to retort, he holds me firmly against him, his lips barely brushing mine.

"I have been waiting for my match and mate for years, and you intrigue me, little one," he murmurs.

Ashton places his lips on mine, gently angling my head to the side as his warm tongue slowly parts my lips. I captivatingly open my mouth to taste him, and he takes control of our first kiss just as I expected he would. Though I have not laid with a man, I have kissed a few, but this kiss is powerful yet tender, exciting, and scary—all at once. He pulls back, looks into my eyes, and smiles. I am in so much trouble; he is dangerous in many ways, but I am intrigued and wonder what it would be like to be with him.

A few of his warriors return, and he steps back from me. My face turns beet red. His silent sidekick approaches, quietly say something to Ashton, and walks away.

He steps toward me, saying, "I have urgent business to attend to, little one. I will seek you out later this afternoon. I have truly enjoyed our sparring match and look forward to our next round."

He turns and leaves, leaving me feeling elated and empty. Why did I let him kiss me like that? He probably does this wooing with any female he wants. I shake my head and start looking for a way back home.

I find Finn back in his stall and ask if he has found anything helpful to get us back home.

Finn replies, *"Evidently, there is a time travel portal in the forest we ended up in. I have no idea how it works or why we were pulled into one."*

Interesting.

"I will try to obtain more information from Ashton this evening. He told me he is half-Elven, so he must know more about these portals."

Finn adds, *"Do you know the one warrior you call Ashton's sidekick? He is following you."*

I immediately take a look around me but see no one.

Finn continues, *"He is leaning against the castle wall in the shadows, talking with a female, but he watches you. Be careful."*

"Thanks, Finn. I will watch out for him. Do you need to shift soon?"

Finn says, *"Not yet. I will let you know."*

I groom, feed, and water Finn, and he sees the dappled gray mare out of her stall and trots over to her. I take my leave and decide to explore the castle grounds and interior. The grounds are tidy, and the warriors appear to be well-disciplined. Various women cook, clean, and garden. Stonemasons are working on various areas of the castle walls.

I find a spot beside a small pond to sit and relax briefly. Multiple flowers are in full bloom, and the trees sway to a light breeze. It is truly beautiful and quiet here until I hear a twig snap behind me. I immediately jump up and start running toward the sound but find nothing—no tracks, no animals, nothing. Walking back to my spot, my mind wanders to Ashton, and again, I wonder what it would be like to have such a man as my own.

I decided to swim in the pond; it is a secluded spot, and the water looks inviting. I remove my mail, leave my chemise on, and wade into the water. The water is warm, and I float on my back, looking at the blue sky and clouds, and my thoughts are quiet. I turn over and dive underwater, enjoying the feel of the water on my skin and hair.

As I swim, I feel a presence nearby. I swim to the edge of the pond to look around cautiously and see Ashton striding toward the pond. His eyes are intense, following my every move.

"Enjoying the water?" he asks, a smirk playing on his lips.

Caught off guard, I nod. "It's peaceful here."

He steps closer, and his gaze enduring. "You seem troubled. Is there something I can help you with?"

I hesitated and then decided to take a chance. "Actually, yes. Finn mentioned a time travel portal in the forest. Do you know anything about it?"

Ashton's expression turns serious. "I've heard rumors, but they are just that—rumors. However, if a portal does exist, it could explain how you ended up here."

Ashton decides to take a chance as well and says, "I know you and your companions are from an Elven realm. Your sword's enchantments, the craftsmanship of your mail, and your expert swordsmanship all point to a place not of this realm."

I can't shake the feeling that there's more to Ashton than meets the eye. His half-elven heritage, knowledge of portals, and protective nature make him a mystery I am eager to unravel. Perhaps in this process, I might find a way back home or discover a new path entirely.

"Thank you for your honesty. I appreciate it."

He smiles softly. "You're welcome, Anwen. We will find a way for you to return home."

I nod and turn and swim toward the other side of the pond.

As I surface in the water, Ashton says, "Would you mind if I join you?" I should tell him no, but instead, I say, "If you wish to swim in your pond, who am I to tell you no?" He smiles and starts slowly removing his mail.

I cannot help but watch him; he is a fine male. He is down to his briefs, which snugly cover him from his lower waist to his knees. His chest and arms are muscular, and a trail of dark hair travels down his abdomen. I like how his body forms a V shape from his hips and down—my eyes stop on, oh, by the gods, that is impressive. My eyes dart immediately back up to his face, and his eyes lock onto mine as he walks into the water.

He swims to the other side of the pond, spreads his arms on the pond bank, and puts his head back, closing his eyes. I start lazily swimming around the pond, wondering why I am so attracted to this male when others rarely gain my interest.

Suddenly, I feel hands around my waist, gently pulling me toward him. He settles me against him, and he whispers, "I cannot stop thinking of you. Is it the same for you?"

"No." I will not admit this to him, but I have thought about him a lot.

Ashton is licking the outside of my ear now—then I feel him gently sucking on it, and all thought has left me.

Ashton says, "Liar, I know you are as attracted to me as I am to you. Why do you fight it?"

I decide I have had enough of this torturous business and swim away from Ashton to the shore. I stand up on the edge of the pond and deny everything I feel for this captivating male.

He starts slowly swimming toward me and smiles, his eyes dropping to my chest and back to my eyes; he says, "You cannot hide your mating arousal; your body is responding to my touch and voice, your pupils enlarge, and your nipples are hard peaks asking for my attention, little one."

Elves are promiscuous by nature; we do not view sharing our bodies with whomever we want as wrong until they are mated. I have never found any male who has made me the least interested until now. When a male elf has found his true mate, he becomes very protective and will challenge any male seen as a threat. Elf males and females, once mated, will only want to be intimately involved with their true mate. When the mating bond is completed, they are mated for life.

This male scares me. I cannot control our interactions. He surprises me and is my equal in everything. He is a challenge, and I don't want to lose my heart to a rogue. I start putting on my mail, erecting my protective walls around my heart again. I turn away, say nothing, and keep walking.

Ashton watches me leave and realizes that she is fighting our attraction. Not to be coy, but she seems afraid to accept his offered affection. She fights against the mating call. He decides to continue using physical attraction to break down those barriers. He would prove she could trust him with her heart.

Deep in thought, I enter the castle's main hall and look up to see a beautiful blonde female who is tall, has almost elven features, is wearing a stunning blue gown, and is staring at me.

The female walks toward me and says, "Who are you?"

Rude, but whatever, "I am Anwen Elwen of the House Elwen, who are you?"

She responds, "I am Sheenal of Moors Keep and betrothed to Ashton. Why are you in his keep, wearing mail and wet?"

Well, it looks like I was right not to get involved with the two-timing rogue; I am pissed now. I say, "It is none of your business what I do or wear."

She looks shocked, and I turn away, trudging up the stairs to my room to lick my wounds and try to figure out how I will get home as soon as possible. I mind-speak with Finn: *"If I ever start talking like a princess, you have permission to roast me."* Finn laughs.

As I climb the stairs, I feel someone behind me and turn to see Sidekick staring at me. I say, "I am getting tired of you spying on me; what do you want?"

He says, "I am not spying on you. Ashton is concerned about your safety, so now I am your bodyguard."

Oh, for the love of gods, "I do not need you as my bodyguard, and I will set Ashton straight on that shortly."

Sidekick raises an eyebrow, seemingly unfazed by my anger. "My name is Banoff," he says quietly.

"And whether you want it or not, I am here to ensure your safety. Orders from Ashton."

I glare at him. "Fine, Banoff. You can follow me if you must, but don't expect me to make it easy for you."

He nods slightly, a hint of a smile playing on his lips. "Understood."

He tells me, "There's intrigue brewing in this kingdom, Anwen, and Ashton is deep in the thick of it. It's not safe for you to wander alone. Sheenal isn't betrothed to Ashton, despite her wishes and perhaps her convincing herself otherwise. Just be wary of her; she's got a streak of spite."

I raise an eyebrow. "Since when did you become so talkative?"

Banoff chuckles warmly, his eyes twinkling. "I see why Ashton is intrigued with you. If you have any questions, just let me know."

I smirk playfully. "How about not running off to Ashton with every little thing you see or hear about me?"

His smile remains, though he shakes his head. "I'm afraid that's impossible, and you know it."

"Fair enough. Can you at least show me where the forest lies and some good spots for Finn to stretch his legs? I need a break from these castle walls, and Finn needs his freedom."

Banoff nods approvingly. "Finn's a fine horse. I'd be honored to show you around, Anwen. The forest has secrets worth exploring."

"Thank you, Banoff. Since you're close to Ashton, I figured you might know a thing or two about Elven customs."

He nods thoughtfully. "I'm human, but Ashton's upbringing ensured I understand their ways."

"About Ashton's family... Are they away?" I inquire gently.

He runs a hand through his hair, a shadow passing over his face. "No, they're gone. Both his parents have passed."

"I'm sorry to hear that," I offer sincerely. Banoff nods in acknowledgment.

"Does anyone else in Ashton's castle know about Elven traditions?" I press on.

He pauses, then responds carefully, "No one else knows. Ashton and I keep that knowledge close. He must trust you deeply to share such a secret."

"I would never put him at risk," I assure him. "But I'm curious. In Eldoria, we're taught there are no half-breeds. How did Ashton come to be?"

As if on cue, Banoff disappears, and Ashton appears on the stairs below, startling me. His voice is low and intimate as he says, "It's true; I am a half-breed. Does that bother you?"

I meet his gaze squarely. "Of course not. Your arrogance and habit of appearing out of nowhere is annoying, though. But your secret is safe with me."

"Good," he murmurs, a hint of amusement in his tone.

"For this half-breed, arrogant, and annoying male is chasing after a beautiful elf who I hope will realize how much I care for her."

I roll my eyes, unable to suppress a smile. "And how can you care so much when we've just met? You presume too much about my feelings."

Ashton steps closer, his eyes intense yet warm. "Because I see you, Anwen. I see your strength, your doubts, and your fierce independence. And I can't help but care."

His words catch me off guard, stirring emotions I hadn't expected. "I've been alone for so long," I admit softly.

He reaches out, his touch gentle as he cups my cheek. "You don't have to be alone anymore."

I am emotionally overwhelmed with his tenderness, which I am not used to. I decided to distance myself and say, "Being alone is better than being a conquest for rogue warriors."

Ashton remains silent, his eyes narrowing, and says, "You do enjoy challenging me, and I am up to it, little one,"

I instinctively press back against the wall to put some space between us.

He moves closer and puts one hand on each side of my head, leaning into me as his lips descend to my neck, tracing a slow path as he licks and lightly nips. One of his hands takes mine, intertwines our fingers, and puts them over his heart. With a firmer bite on my neck, pleasure grows through me and stirring sensations I have never experienced. His teeth hold me gently while his other hand caresses my ear and sends shivers down my spine. Instinctively, my hips moved against him, seeking more of his touch.

Suddenly, Ashton withdraws, his deep voice cutting through the charged air.

"You can deny it all you want." he says, his gaze intense, "but your body betrays you. From the moment we met, I knew you were meant for me. I desire you, and I will make you mine. Keep resisting if you must, but I will win your heart."

With those words between us, he turns and descends the stairs, leaving me standing there in physical frustration. Why did I let this dominant man affect me so deeply? Anger welled within me at my lack of control, yet if he wanted a battle, he had just got one.

FIVE

Ambush in the Forest

The discovery of the portal is a gut punch. One minute, I shiver in soaking armor; the next, my imagination is on fire. Ashton's forest isn't just creepy anymore, but it crackles with secrets! That doorway connects with forgotten magic and promising answers I crave. My brain goes into overdrive – what triggers these hidden Portals of Destiny? A specific invocation? A rare flower blooming under a full moon? Maybe even a sassy one-liner delivered with the right amount of swagger? That last one is probably out, but the frustration is real.

I need answers more than a warm bath, though that does sound mighty tempting; I throw on dry clothes under my armor, feeling the familiar weight of metal settle on my shoulders. As I stomp down the stairs, ready to head back to the forest with a vengeance, Sheenal appears suddenly like an angry snake. Her eyes hold enough venom to melt steel, and her words are filled with disrespect and something that suspiciously resembles possessiveness. "Chasing after my betrothed," she sneers, "how unbecoming of a lowly warrior like yourself."

Ugh. Here we go again.

I let out a sigh that could fog up a dragon's nostril and stop dead in my tracks. Then, with a spark of defiance igniting in my chest, I march right up to her, stopping so close I can practically count the spite freckles on her nose. "Listen closely, Princess Perfect," I growl, my voice is low and dangerous. "He isn't your betrothed, and your claws would look much better without fresh battle scars." The satisfaction of seeing her eyes widen is worth the risk of a catfight. But before she can throw a tantrum, I can't deal with this anymore. I turn and leave her sputtering insults behind.

As I approach, Finn greets me with a spirited whinny that instantly lifts my spirits. A smile spreads across my face, washing away all my worries. He's finishing his hay, and I step into his stall, running my hands over his sleek coat. *I can tell something's on your mind,* Finn says with a knowing look.

Maynard is absorbed in her feathers and perched nearby on a stall board and taunts, *She's irritated by her warrior, again.*

I can't help but laugh heartily. Being clear-headed is my safe place. The comforting sounds of horses' whinnies soothe me, and the smell of hay relaxes me. I prepare my horse with a confident smile for the journey ahead. The secrets of the forest await, and I, the lowly warrior, is about to become a legend. I grab Finn's gear as I explain my latest plan to both of my trusted companions. I lead him out of his stall and swing into the saddle as Maynard takes flight. Finn eases into a slow canter with a very gentle bump as we depart from the castle. I guide him back toward the woods, savoring the warm sun on my face and the rich scents of the forest.

After a brief ride, Maynard swoops down with news of our progress, *"Looks like our plan is successful!"* I quickly looked back, a wave of relief washing over me as I saw Banoff. He sat tall and proud on his incredible warhorse. The horse's coat was a shiny copper color, and its mane danced in the wind. He rides closer with a big and warm grin, crinkling the corners of his eyes. He understands how nervous I am about being in the thick forest. He isn't saying anything, but he pulls his horse up next to me and gives me a reassuring nod. Then, he takes the lead. I follow close behind him, glad for the company. His broad back seems like a strong anchor in the confusing wilderness. Finn and I settle into a comfortable pace, enjoying the rhythmic lope as we travel farther into the wilderness.

We walk for another mile in complete silence, except for the steady sound of the horses' hooves and the leaves crunching under our feet. I am highly strung. This thick forest, with all its hidden endangerment, felt like a hazard to animals itself. Banoff suddenly stops his horse. He raises his hand in a fist with his fingers spread out, which is a heads-up to be careful.

A burst of energy shot through me. Finn and I look up quickly and scan the whole forest frantically. Every sound of leaves seems louder, and every moving shadow looks like a threat. Finn also gets tense. His ears perk up like antennas, and his eyes, which are usually playful, turn hard. Then, we hear a low whistle. It is Maynard. She spoke very quietly from somewhere above us, and what she said confirmed our worst fears. *"There's a patrol of four knights. They're coming from the southwest."* The sound of horses' hooves is faint but gets louder quickly. There are muffle voices coming from through the trees. The sounds of horses and men talking.

I whisper to Finn, *"What could they be patrolling for?"* Finn's ears twitch as he listens closely; he says, *"They're looking for a witch,"* his mind speaks. *"A powerful witch who possesses combat skills, fighting with the strength and prowess of a seasoned warrior. She also has the extraordinary ability to control and influence the minds of others, bending their will to her own."*

I chuckle softly, *"Now that's a trick I'd like to learn."*

I almost laugh out loud nervously, but I stop myself by biting my lip. The absurdity of the situation is almost too much to handle, and a nervous giggle threatens to escape, but I manage to keep it at bay. I let my mind wander to a fantasy, a daydream that has often brought me comfort and strength. A strong, magical woman, her presence is commanding, and her powers are undeniable, making her way confidently in a world dominated by men. She strides with purpose, her head held high, undeterred by the obstacles and prejudices that litter her path. The image of her with her fierce determination and unyielding spirit makes me rebellious and empowered.

Maynard assures us that this is the only patrol in the vicinity. With a swift hand signal from Banoff, we veer off the trail and into the shelter of the trees, successfully evading the knights. "It's unusual for patrols to be sent out looking for witches," Banoff muses. "I need to inform Ashton about this."

We press deeper into the forest, the canopy above us growing denser as Maynard soars overhead, ever watchful for danger. Banoff slows his mount and turns to me. "I want to scout ahead. If you need help, can you mimic a bird call loudly?"

"No problem," I assure him. "Do the same if you run into trouble." Banoff smiles, a reassuring glint in his eyes, before riding ahead and disappearing from view.

Finn lets me know he's nearing his shift time. I acknowledge it, *"We'll find a safe spot soon."* I promise while mentally preparing for our next move in the endangered forest.

As we round a corner on the trail, Maynard's urgent shrill call pierces the air—a sign of an imminent attack. In an instant, a masked black-clad assassin leaps from a tree, aiming for Finn's head. Finn rears back, and I instinctively call Ashbringer to my hand. From the opposite side, another assassin springs from the shadows and knocks me from Finn's back.

I don't resist the momentum; instead, I roll just before hitting the ground, as my body moves with practiced ease. Finn's assailant grabs his bridle only to receive a powerful strike to the stomach. As I rise, the second assassin hurls two throwing stars at me. Ashbringer deflects them with a swift command. Seizing my moment, I direct Ashbringer to slash the attacker's biceps and neutralize any further threat.

A glance confirms Finn's dominance—he has his attacker by the shoulder, shaking him like a rag doll. Refocusing on my foe, I see his arms hanging uselessly at his sides and take Ashbringer back in my grip. I let out a sharp bird whistle, signaling Banoff, then subdue my assassin with speed, binding his hands and legs with leather strips from my pockets.

Suddenly, pain sears through my right shoulder—a thrown star. There's a third assassin! Yanking the star out, I distressfully scan the area but see no one. Finn, such a vigilant, drops his assailant and pins him to the ground with a decisive stomp to the stomach.

"Was the star poisoned?" Finn asks, his voice tinged with concern.

"I'm not sure yet," I reply, still scanning the area for the elusive third assassin. My eyes catch sight of Banoff charging in fast around the

trailing corner. He dismounts rapidly and secures Finn's conquered attacker before rushing over to us.

"Are you both okay?" Banoff inquires, his eyes darting between me and Finn.

"There was a third assassin," I inform him, my voice steady despite the growing unease. "We haven't found him yet, but we're fine for now."

Banoff immediately begins scouring the surroundings, searching for the hidden threat. I motion for Finn to come closer, but I feel uneasy. *"I'm feeling dizzy and nauseous,"* I admit.

"We need to return to the castle quickly and hope their healer can provide a counter potion."

Finn begins to shift into his dragon form without any hesitation. His transformation is both awe-inspiring and speedy, his size and beauty magnified as scales replace hair. He finishes his shift and extends a massive leg toward me. With as much speed as I can muster, I climb up his leg and settle onto his broad back.

Banoff reappears and stops abruptly; his body shows signs of tension and alertness. Finn roars a powerful sound that reverberates through the forest. He launches us into the air with a mighty push from his muscular legs, his wings unfurling majestically as we ascend. Tree limbs crack and snap as we rise, but soon, we are above the shade and heading straight for Ashton's castle. The effects of the drug begin to hit me hard, and I cling tightly to Finn.

"Hang on, Anwen. I'll get help for you," Finn's voice is a reassuring echo in my mind.

As we come near the castle, Finn lowers us into a small grove of trees just outside the walls. I slide off his back, and my legs wobbling beneath me. In a fluid motion, he shifts back into his horse form and gallops toward the castle. Moments later, Ashton appears with his strong arms, lifting me effortlessly.

"What happened?" he asks, his eyes wide open with worry.

"We were ambushed by assassins in the forest," I manage to say. "I was hit with a poisoned throwing star in my shoulder."

Ashton runs inside the castle, shouting for bandages and the healer as he takes the stairs two at a time. He kicks open the door to my room and lays me gently on the bed. My chambermaid is right behind him, preparing water and bandages quickly. His commanding voice is loud as he orders each word, intensifying the headache pounding in my skull. I wish he would lower his voice.

Ashton removed my upper body mail and carefully pulled apart the fabric over the wound to examine it. His worried expression makes me smile despite the pain. "It's not so bad," I assure him, touching his face lightly. "You should have seen what I did to the other guy."

He steps aside and allows my maid to begin cleaning the wound. Another woman enters, carrying herbs and poultices. She gently moves him to get a better look at the injury and asks me a few questions before starting to prepare a potion. He grips my hand tightly and urges the healer to hurry.

A while later, the healer applies a foul-smelling ointment to the wound and wraps it with cloth bandages. Exhaustion washes over me, and my eyelids grow heavy. His hand in mine is the last thing I feel as I drift into a deep, much-needed sleep.

Ashton leaves me in the capable hands of the healer and chambermaid; his heart is beating fast, and his mind is racing with questions. He had been inspecting the castle walls with the stonemasons, discussing future repairs, when Finn came charging at him, neighing loudly and rearing before sprinting in the opposite direction. Realizing Finn was trying to lead him somewhere, Ashton followed, his heart sinking as he found me lying on the ground, still and pale.

Banoff arrived at the castle shortly after finding Ashton in the stables, putting Finn into his stall and removing his tack. He quickly recounted the ambush in the forest and my bravery.

"She was wounded and beat you back to the castle?" Ashton asked quietly, awe and concern in his voice.

Banoff isn't sure Ashton would believe him, but he explains nonetheless, "Both assassins were defeated and tied up. Anwen said there was one more, and neither of them was injured. I started scouting the immediate area for the third assassin. When I came back around a corner in the trail, I saw Finn shapeshifting from horse form into a large black and red dragon. She climbed onto his back, and he took off. I take full responsibility for failing to protect her."

Ashton pauses while grooming Finn, his hands freezing as he listens intently. He then quietly asks Finn, "Is this true, Finn?" He turns his head, looking directly into Ashton's eyes, and nods. Ashton steps back, glancing at Banoff, who shrugs as if to say, "See what I mean."

A realization dawns on Ashton, and he recalls the shadow of a dragon's head he had seen around Finn when he first met Anwen and Finn. He placed a hand on his mane and said, "Thank you, Finn, for saving her life."

He snorts softly and resumes eating his hay, the moment of tension dissolving into the familiar sounds of the stable.

Ashton and Banoff walk inside the castle. He tells Banoff to wait for him in the study and climbs the stairs to Anwen's room to check on her. She is sleeping peacefully, and the healer assures him that the potion will draw out the poison, though she needs plenty of rest. He gets closer to her, gently kisses Anwen's forehead, and whispers, "Rest, Anwen. You are safe here." He leaves the room quietly and tells his Knight of Arms to arrange for a guard to stand outside her door with strict orders that only the healer maid and he can enter.

He returns downstairs and enters his private study. He goes to his spirits cabinet and pours two drinks. Both men sit in chairs before the fireplace, sipping their drinks as they discuss the events in the forest. Banoff reveals that one assassin is killed; he seems to have bled out quickly from a torso wound. The other assassin is brought back and is now in the castle dungeon. Although he knows Ashton will want answers from him soon. They are still in search of the third assassin, who remains elusive.

SIX

Unraveling the Threads

The next morning starts with dark shadows in the sky, casting an eerie gloom over the castle grounds. It feels as though something unbearable is about to seize everyone's minds. Ashton and Banoff begin the interrogation in the dim dungeon chamber; their expressions are tense, and their minds racing with the troubling confessions they pry from the assassin's reluctant lips. The light from the torch moves and creates spooky or strange shadows on the wet stone walls, creating an oppressive atmosphere that matches the gravity of the situation. The air is thick with the feeling of fear and desperation from both the prisoner and the interrogators.

Ashton looks directly into the assassin's eyes, a man with a gaunt face and eyes that flare with defiance and terror. The assassin's wrists are tied with heavy iron chains, and a drop of sweat runs down his forehead, showing his stress. They can smell his fear. Ashton leans forward and whispers into his ear with a low and dangerous voice.

"Do you understand that you will not leave here alive? We can make your passing difficult or quick, your choice." Ashton demands, his tone making it clear that there's no room for evasion. "Who sent you? What are your orders?" Banoff stands beside him, imposing a big and physically strong body with his arms folded across his chest. His face looks serious, his jaw tight, and he keeps staring at the Jesuit assassin without turning away. The silence in the chamber is broken only by the distant dripping of water and the Jesuit assassin's ragged breathing. The Jesuit assassin hesitates, his eyes moving around the room as if he is planning to escape. He speaks with a trembling voice, "Father Thorne... informed the Pope of the witch you harbor. The Pope ordered us to capture the girl, Anwen. He believes she practices forbidden magic." Ashton's expressions are stern, and he clenches his fists at his sides. "And what does he plan to do with her?" he asks with a barely controlled voice.

The Jesuit assassin gulps nervously with dreadful eyes, "He plans to interrogate her and extract her secrets. He wants to make her an example to instill fear in those who oppose him." Banoff steps forward, "Who else is involved?" he asks with a low growl voice, "How many more are coming?" The Jesuit assassin's determination breaks, and he begins to speak willingly, spitting out the words rapidly. "There are others, many others. Father Thorne and the Pope have spies everywhere, even within your own ranks. They are determined to root out all who defy them." Ashton and Banoff exchange a worried glance because the danger is greater than they imagined, and time is running out already.

Further questioning reveals no additional information. The prisoner is dispatched quickly. His head is displayed on a pike beside the road entering the forest. The pike has Ashton's banner attached, which blows gently in the breeze. Ashton wants to be clear about his actions toward anyone who threatens those under his care.

Father Gabriel Thorne's and Pope Paul V's names hang in the air heavily—both well-respected leaders in the Roman Catholic Church who are now involved in a sinister witch hunt. Ashton realizes he must devise a plan quickly to protect Anwen and counter their sinister dark schemes.

"I still can't believe it, Banoff. Father Gabriel Thorne and the Pope. Of all people, I never suspected them to be behind this madness. How could those so respected be involved in such a heinous plot?"

"I know, Ashton. It's hard to wrap my head around it, too. But the evidence is undeniable. The Jesuit assassin's information makes sense and explains why Anwen is being hunted now. Father Thorne manipulates his position in the church for his sinister purposes."

Ashton says, "An informant from House Lionsway... it has to be someone close to us and someone who knows Anwen well enough to betray her. This betrayal will not be tolerated. No traitor will continue to hide within my castle walls and threaten those I care for. "We're all in danger. Father Thorne's lies provided to the Pope can have a vast influence. If he manages to convince the church that she is a witch, it's only a matter of time before they come for her—and us." We need to act quickly. We can't just sit and wait for them to strike. She is vulnerable, and we can't let her fall into their hands. She's done nothing wrong—practicing magic isn't a crime, but to them, it's a death sentence."

"I agree. We have to find out who the informant is and stop them before they can do more damage. And we need to figure out a way to protect her and ourselves. Do you think we can trust anyone in the castle?"

"Right now, I don't know. I am unable to trust anyone and risk anything. We have to be cautious, Banoff. Everyone is a suspect until they are proven otherwise. The stakes are too high for us to make any mistakes."

"So, what's the plan? How do we proceed?"

"First, we need to get Anwen to understand the situation and provide protection. Then, we start our own investigation. We'll question everyone if we have to, but we will find out who betrayed us."

"And Father Thorne? How do we deal with him?"

"We will expose them all. We will gather enough evidence to prove his and the Pope's corruption and present it to Queen Elizabeth. It's a long shot, but it might be the only way to stop them. We must stay one step ahead of Father Thorne and his reporting to the Pope. Then gather intel on the Pope and stop his assassins."

"I'll start making arrangements for Anwen's safety immediately. I will secure the castle and forest and start making inquiries for intel on Father Thorne and the Pope."

"Good. Be careful because we can't afford to lose now. This fight is just beginning, and we need to be ready for whatever comes next."

"Understood. There will be no place evil can hide that we will not find them." Ashton nods with a determined look in his eyes. They both know the road ahead will be perilous, but they are ready to face it. They unite to protect Anwen and his people. They would uncover the truth behind the treachery that threatens them all.

Ashton's jaw clenches as he acquires the weight of this knowledge. The Church's relentless hunt for supposed witches and labeling them as agents of evil isn't just a myth—it's a harsh truth. Innocent people are in danger, caught in the sights of a power-hungry group that wants to control everything. Accusations are spreading like wildfire, making everyone afraid if they're suspected of having magical powers. He feels a deep burden by the solemnity of the situation. He walks back and forth in the room, thinking relentlessly about this. The Church's mission isn't merely about finding heretics; it's a deliberate effort to gather power and silent dissent. They label anyone with even a bit of magical knowledge as a threat, portraying them as servants of darkness who are destined for punishment by fire.

Anwen's safety and everyone's lives are now at serious risk due to being squarely on Father Thorne's radar. Ashton knows he must act swiftly and is determined to uncover the castle's traitor. Ashton has Banoff gathering his most trusted advisors to meet in the war room for planning, which is crucial in this dangerous situation.

The atmosphere on the castle grounds is tense as Ashton readies himself to confront the imminent danger. His heart feels heavy with the responsibility and urgency to protect those he cares about. The usually bustling courtyard is eerily quiet, and each stone seems to hold its breath in anticipation.

In the war room, lit by flickering candles, Ashton gathers his trusted advisors around maps spread out on the table. Their faces show earnestness, reflecting the gravity of the situation.

"We must find the leak," Ashton says firmly. "Someone within these walls is giving information to Father Thorne and putting us all at risk. Banoff, you have to fortify our defenses. Increase patrols and set up watchtowers along the perimeter. We can't afford any surprises."

Banoff nods grimly. "Consider it done. I'll ensure no one comes or goes unnoticed."

Ashton turns to the group, his gaze sweeping their faces. "Prepare for the worst. Father Thorne now has the Pope's influence, and it is extensive. The Pope won't hesitate to strike with his Jesuit assassins. Stay alert and watch each other's backs. Together, we will endure this evil storm."

Meanwhile, I wake up feeling like I've been trampled by a wagon but grateful to be alive. The chambermaid brings me a light meal and prepares a soothing bath, which will revive my spirits. After eating and enjoying the warm bath, I feel much better. As I descend the staircase later, I cross paths with Ashton, who is coming up and looks surprised to see me out of bed so soon.

"Why are you out of bed already?" Ashton asks with concern, gently picking me up and guiding me toward my room without letting me speak. I give him a defiant glare as he settles me into a chair. I promptly stand up and head back toward the stairs.

"If you promise to take it easy for a few days, I'll share what I've learned with you, and we can start planning," Ashton proposes, catching up to me and leading me gently downstairs toward the study. I reluctantly agree, descend the stairs again, and slip into the comforting atmosphere of Ashton's study.

Ashton finds himself oddly fulfilled by ensuring my comfort. I deeply inhale his scent; it is on everything in the room, and it soothes me. He updates me on the unsettling events threatening their safety as they settle into his study.

"My sources have uncovered several alarming plots," Ashton begins, his tone serious. "The persecution of women being accused of witchcraft has been intensifying greatly. It begins with Pope Paul V's declaration of Queen Elizabeth as a heretic, excommunicating her through a Papal Bull. This act releases Catholics from their allegiance to her and urges them to remove her from the throne. The Church aims to eliminate any opposition to their dominance and establish themselves as the supreme authority."

I listen intently, my brow furrowing with concern. "So, they're using accusations of witchcraft to solidify their power?" I ask, my voice tinged with disbelief.

"Yes," Ashton confirms with a troubled expression. "Father Thorne and his allies are using fear to control the masses. They believe any hint of magic is a threat to their authority."

I shake my head with anger and sadness in my eyes. "It's injustice!" I mutter. "To persecute innocent people for their beliefs or abilities—it's barbaric."

"I agree," Ashton says softly, reaching out to squeeze my hand reassuringly. "We can't let them succeed. We have to find a way to expose their motives and protect those they target."

I nod with evident determination. "So, what's our next move?"

"We need to gather more information," Ashton replies, his gaze steady. We'll need to be cautious and strategic."

I nod again, a plan forming in my mind. "And what about the traitor in the castle? Do you have any lead?"

"Not yet," he hesitates, "But I won't rest until we uncover their identity." He sighs heavily, the weight of the situation evident in his voice. "Father Thorne must have told the Pope everything, leading to this planned mission to capture you and Finn."

Ashton's words hang in the air, describing the tough situation they're in and the ruthless enemies they're up against.

The more I grasp the grim truth, the more anger wells up inside me. "How could the Pope and Father Thorne justify harming innocent people to gain power and riches? Eldoria abandoned organized religion after seeing its destructive impact in endless wars driven by greed and control. Instead, they revere the Earth's elements, pledging to protect them from exploitation. This belief nurtures Eldoria in fostering prosperity and equality among its people."

I bluntly try to discover the traitor within the castle walls. "I've been thinking that Sheenal seems like the likely suspect with her sly manner."

"You're right. She's been too quiet lately. I'm planning to coax a confession from her about her connection to Father Thorne." Says Ashton.

"And what about Banoff's patrols? Any signs of more infiltrators or suspicious activities on our grounds?" I ask.

"Not yet. He's keeping a close watch, but everything's quiet so far. We need to stay alert."

I clench my fists and my determination solidifies as I decide to leave the study room. I excuse myself from Ashton and seek out Maynard and Finn to discuss the current situation of Father Thorne and the Pope. I refuse to let the forces of power and manipulation win, not at the expense of innocent lives or their principles.

Before I reach them, Finn's voice echoes softly in my mind, filled with concern and support. *"How are you feeling? Why are you up already?"*

My mental voice responds firmly, *"I'm getting stronger, Finn."* I quickly brief him on the latest developments. Turning to Maynard, she asks, *"Can you keep track of the priest's movements and report back daily?"*

Maynard nods assuredly. *"Yes, I'll monitor his routines and watch for anything suspicious in our area."*

"Finn," I continue, my tone serious, *"you need to lay low. The Jesuit assassin who escaped knows about your transformation. They'll be searching for you."* Finn nods solemnly, agreeing to stay within the safety of the castle walls and keep an eye out for any threats.

I glance up to see Ashton striding in my direction, looking at me soberly with a half-smile. "Discussing plans with your friends?" he asks gently.

"Yes," I say. "I'm concerned for your safety and that of my friends. Father Thorne and the Pope's Jesuits are determined to capture Finn and me. Now, your association with us puts you at risk in this witch hunt."

Ashton nods resolutely. "I've taken measures to strengthen the castle and protect our surroundings, including you and your friends."

I lock eyes with him; my voice is steadfast. "I swear that the darkness lurking within these powerful institutions of religion will not prevail. We are Paladins; we protect those who cannot do so themselves. Righteousness will win against those who worship evil. The light will conquer them."

Right after saying that, I thought to myself, "What other challenges will tomorrow bring now?"

SEVEN

Popes and Jesuits

The sun rises, and its golden light shines on the old, cobblestone streets. Father Thorne can barely contain his excitement. Today is not just any day—it is the day of his greatest achievement. His heart pounds like a war drum, echoing in the early morning.

He whispers to himself with a deep breath, "This is it. This is the moment I've been waiting for."

He walks purposefully through the narrow alleyways; his hands are trembling with excitement and exhilaration. He holds the parchment tightly, and the ink is still fresh from the night before. The letter, addressed to the Pope, is a declaration of his incredible discovery of a real witch and not just any witch—a witch with a dragon. His mind races with the possibilities. The Pope will surely be astounded by such news. Thorne already envisioned the scene: *The grand cathedral, the high altar, and the Pope's solemn nod of approval.*

"Oh, how they will sing my praises," he murmurs, a victorious grin on his face.

The weight of the bishop's robes seems almost tangible to him now, as if he can feel the heavy ornate robes resting on his shoulders. The thought of stepping out from the shadows of his tiny parish and into the grandeur of power and position within the church gives him a thrilling purpose.

And the sun fully rises, warming the town, and Father Thorne's era of glory begins. A simple priest like him is about to become a legend.

The Pope informed him that he had personally directed his Jesuit warriors, also known as "God's warriors," on a crucial mission of capturing Anwen and Finn. Among the Christian clergy, knowledge of the Jesuit sect of the Roman Catholic Church is sparse, with many unaware of their existence or their sacred vows binding them to fulfill any duty assigned by the Pontiff—missions that demand unwavering dedication and sacrifice.

Meanwhile, the Jesuits meticulously observe the daily routines and security measures at House Lionsway focusing intently on me and Finn. It seems inevitable that they will soon devise a strategy to apprehend both of us. Ashton Everett is no less a target in Father Thorne's eyes due to his superiority. To Thorne, Ashton epitomizes the same sinfulness and heresy he attributes to me. Ashton amassed land and wealth when he joined the Knights Templars and the Crusades. Thorne views Ashton as a valuable target.

Father Thorne plans and envisions a scheme coming together for their downfall. He is going to issue a proclamation throughout the town depicting a hand-drawn drawing based on Sheenal's description of me. This poster will offer a big reward for catching me, stirring up people's desire for money and fear of consequences. Simultaneously, the Jesuits are bound by their oath to obey the Pontiff's commands, close in on their targets, tightening the noose around me, Finn, and Ashton alike.

Just before dawn, Thorne gets ready to start his plan; he feels a surge of anticipation and determination. It's not just about chasing a witch and her friends; it's about seeking power and respect, a chance to rise from his early struggles to a position of authority in the church. It's time for a visit to House Lionsway, which brings him closer to the victory that he awaits.

Finn and I are restless. We understand the importance of laying low, but it goes against our instincts to remain in hiding. To keep our skills sharp, I practice weapons training daily, which helps me feel calm and focused. Ashton recognizes I need the company to practice with, so he often joins me for sparring matches. In the evening, we relax by playing chess and talking about our lives, dreams, and what worries us. The more I learn about Ashton's life and experiences, the deeper my admiration grows.

In the middle of all the tension, Ashton has a clear realization. He confronts Sheenal, suspecting her involvement in accusing me of witchcraft, Father Thorne. She fiercely denies it, but Ashton is firm about his convictions, and he orders her to leave his castle immediately. The atmosphere feels tense and uncomfortable as Sheenal departs, leaving behind a feeling of uncertainty that hangs in the air.

We're waiting for Father Thorne or the Pope to make their first move. The tension is concrete and palpable, like a pause before a storm. We're all on edge, wondering what they'll do next, and suddenly, unexpected news arrives that Father Thorne is arriving and seeking a meeting with Ashton. I excuse myself from the room with the feeling of frustration and anxiousness. Keeping secrets is hard—I hate the constant hiding and not knowing what will happen next.

I am pacing back and forth in my room. My thoughts are jumbled and troubling. How will Ashton handle the situation when Father Thorne comes? What does the priest intend to discuss? I am sure that Father Thorne is planning something to harm us all. I know Ashton will handle this problem with his strength and determination and guard our place.

Father Thorne is brought into his study room. Ashton stares at the clergy in a serious and deliberately intimidating manner. He stands tall and continues staring at the clergyman with a bit of controlled disdain, silently showing his dominance. He turns toward the window without uttering a word with his arms folded behind his back and calmly greets Father Thorne, "Good day, Father Thorne. How may I assist you?"

Father Thorne feels a knot of nerves tighten in his stomach and a familiar sensation he loathes. Ashton's commanding stature and prestigious title always make him uneasy, but now the tables have turned. The accusation of witchcraft is hanging over them, and Father Thorne feels powerful, wielding it like a righteous weapon against this supposed heretic.

His voice trembles slightly as he speaks, "Are you aware of the grave accusations concerning a witch has seen on your castle grounds and in the surrounding forest? This is a matter of utmost seriousness and suggests you are harboring a witch and thus implicating yourself as a heretic. Pope Paul V has already been informed that your actions will have consequences. What do you have to say in defense of these allegations?"

Ashton remains serene, constantly gazing outside the window, and he responds steadily, "I have not received any formal accusation from the Pope. I advise you to be careful, Father Thorne. Your insinuations are serious, and I have little tolerance for baseless threats. It would be wise for you to reconsider your stance and leave before my patience runs out enough to challenge you for the slander against my name. I doubt you would find a duel to your advantage, Father, do you?"

"What! Well, I didn't mean to... never mind." The tension in the room crackles like a storm is about to break. Father Thorne hesitates, and his confidence falters in the face of Ashton's demeanor. He feels the precarious balance of power shifting, unsure of what will happen next as a heavy silence settles between them. Flustered and defeated, Father Thorne spins on his heel and exits the study with humiliation.

As he walks away from Ashton's imposing presence, frustration gnaws at him. He has done everything within his power, but the next move is out of his hands. For now, he is forced to endure the wait, but his mind is simmering with thoughts of revenge and the hope that soon, the balance of power will shift in his favor.

His thoughts seethe with resentment. His time will come, and he will savor the moment when the Pope finally destroys everything Ashton holds dear.

Yet, a bitter reality tempers his fantasies. The Pope has expressly forbidden Thorne from further involvement in this matter. It is a directive he cannot ignore. Defying the Pope would shatter his ambitions of rising within the church's hierarchy. He has no choice but to bide his time and await further orders.

There was a knock on my door, and Ashton arrived to escort me to dinner. We sit quietly in our usual places, not communicating as the dinner platters are laid out on the table. There is an urge of tension due to Father Thorne's recent visit.

"I still can't believe he had the nerve to come here," I say with a heavy voice of worry. "I'm concerned for my friends and for you, Ashton."

Ashton reaches out gently, placing his hand on my thigh. "We'll be okay, Anwen. We just have to stay vigilant."

I find it impossible to think clearly when he touches me, savoring the sensation of his caresses as we finish our meal.

After dinner, we are going to the study. I walk toward the window, gazing out into the night, and my mind is heavy with thoughts of the powerful forces conspiring against us.

"I don't know how we're going to deal with all of this," I murmur.

Ashton approaches from behind, wrapping his arms around me and pulling me close. "We'll find a way," he says softly, his breath warm against my ear.

I lean into him, and my anxiety momentarily melts away. He brushes my hair aside and nuzzles my ear, then my neck, and I close my eyes, surrendering to the feelings only he can invoke.

"For now, just relax," Ashton whispers, making her acutely aware of his presence.

His tongue and teeth tease the base of my neck while his fingers trace gentle circles around my nipple. A wave of pleasure washes over me, and I think to myself, "Damn, that feels good."

His other hand goes down to my thighs, cupping me firmly before slipping his fingers beneath my dress and seeking out the spot that gives me the most pleasure. I can feel his arousal as he presses his hips against my buttocks; his movements are slow and deliberate. The only sound is of my soft intake of breath as he continues to stimulate me.

I am still figuring out if I can trust him with my body. But the question is whether I can let him into my heart so soon. I know that allowing myself to fall in love with him is risky— it's a big gamble for me. But when he touches me, it sends waves of pleasure through me; I start to wonder if he's worth taking that *risk*.

He whispers, "Stop overthinking." His touch makes me feel warm as he gently turns me around in his arms and kisses me passionately, making our bond deeper.

I eagerly respond, our mouths meeting in a passionate kiss that shows how much we desire each other. He breaks away and gently pulls down the strap of my gown, which reveals a delicate rose-pink nipple. He circles around it with a tender touch, sometimes nibbling and licking, making me moan softly. He repeats his licking and sucking on my opposite breast, causing my pleasure to climb.

He lifts me up effortlessly, carries me to a nearby couch, and seats me on his lap. His hand slips beneath my dress; he finds me hot and wet. He slides his fingers sensuously over my sex, his experience evident as he continues to make me want more. He sucked my breast harder and teased me into a frenzy of sensation.

I feel overwhelmed by the intensity of his ministrations, so tonight, I surrender myself to his promises. I push against his hand, releasing all fears and shyness, giving myself entirely to my "Dark Hair." Looking into his eyes, I see his smile—a silent vow of his contentment in providing me pleasure as he puts his fingers in his mouth and sucks on them. Oh, my gods, this man will make me insane with need.

I nuzzle his neck, craving the taste of his skin, but he restrains me, pressing his body against mine with controlled urgency. He wants to focus on my pleasure only, showing me that he cares for me, which outweighs his desires, too.

I look at him and ask softly, "Is everything alright?"

"I wanted to give you this moment to show you can trust me." He says softly and with sincerity.

His words resonate deeply within my heart, reaffirming the bond we share. Yet, as he holds me close, his touch evoking a potent desire and longing, *I yearn for more*. I know he couldn't commit to this bond until I ultimately gave him my heart.

His fingers move in slow, careful circles around my nipple; his touch is gentle yet possessive. In that intimate moment, he confesses how I have opened his heart like never before. "I've never felt this close to anyone," he murmured. "You make me want to protect, cherish, and love you with all my heart."

I look down, struggling with my own feelings. "I want to believe you," I admit quietly. "To open up to you. But I'm not ready for that yet, my Dark Hair."

He nods, "I understand," he says, his voice steady with patience and devotion. "I can wait until you realize we will be together. But remember this— I will always love you."

He pulls me closer, making my heart beat faster. Can I overcome my worries and fears and concede to love him? This big question echoes in my mind as I look into his eyes, trying to find the answer inside me.

We walk silently down the dimly lit corridor to our rooms. He pauses at my door, a flicker of concern in his eyes as he checks the surroundings for any sign of danger. After he is satisfied that I am safe, he opens the door and leads me inside. Before leaving my room, he kisses me intensely. His hands move with a comforting familiarity, holding my back and gently pulling me closer to him.

He kisses me slow and long as his hands knead my buttocks, pulling them apart, lifting them over and over. He finally lifts his head, kisses my forehead, says, "Goodnight, little one," and walks out the door.

As I lie in bed and fall asleep, I start dreaming of all the delicious things he does to my body. Suddenly, a hand clamps over my mouth and forcefully pulls the covers off. Panic rushes through me as I fight against the person I can't see. They quickly tie my hands and put a gag in my mouth.

I am mentally screaming for help from Finn and Maynard. I gather all of my strength and slam the heels of my hands into the attacker's nose. There's a horrible crunch as blood pours from his nostrils. He grunts in pain but swiftly covers my nose and mouth with a foul-smelling cloth. Fear and adrenaline surge through her veins as she fights for each breath, her limbs becoming heavy and unresponsive. The room spins, her vision blurs, and darkness threatens to engulf her.

The kidnappers debate over whether to seize the horse, but the piercing scream of the terrifying horse and the splintering crash of boards convince them to flee immediately. One of them lifts me onto his back and starts to climb out the window. Meanwhile, the other kidnapper reinforces the door before following his accomplice out the window.

Maynard observes the two men from a distance. One man is carrying me, galloping toward the forest on horseback. She silently tracks their path and relays their direction to Finn.

"Stay with them." Finn directed. *"I'll bring help."*

In the barn, Ashton hears the loud sounds of wood cracking and splintering and hurries to check on Finn. The stallion is in a panic, wrecking his stall; sweat gleams on its neck and sides, and his eyes are wide with dread. Ashton approaches calmly and inquires about the cause. Finn's gaze flicks toward the castle, a harrowing scream escaping his lips before he turns back to Ashton. Ashton bolted toward the castle after understanding the gravity of the situation.

"No, no!" Ashton muttered urgently as he raced up the stairs.

He quickly attempts to open my door, but it is blocked. He beats on the door, calling out my name in desperation. When he receives no answer, he sprints to his room, seizes his sword, and begins hacking at the door. Once inside, he sees blood on the bed and window frame; she is gone, and the window curtain gently blows in the breeze.

He looks out the window and cries my name into the darkness with a sorrowful guttural scream, "Anwen."

EIGHT

Water Dragon

"Where am I?" I think to myself, keeping my eyes closed. My head is spinning, and I'm so confused.

I slowly realize that I am lying on my side with my hands and feet tightly bound. I pretend to be out still and listen. The two males who abducted me are sitting on the ground eating. They are quietly discussing who will be on guard duty and how long they will stay here before heading for *Rome.*

"Rome? What?" I murmur to myself, and my mind races with fear and hesitation.

I suspect Father Thorne is behind this abduction, but the kidnappers have mentioned Rome, which suggests a deeper and more ominous plot involving powerful forces aligned with the Pope himself.

I'm without my sword or horse, although I trust that Maynard is tracking them. I know Ashton and Finn will be coming for me, so I know I must act quickly. I need to buy time to slow down these kidnappers long enough for my friends to catch up. With all my determination, I started to plan my getaway, and I'm aware that my future—including my people—is at stake.

I stir and let out a soft moan, signaling my awakening. One of the Jesuits rises and moves away, presumably to keep watch. The other approaches me swiftly, gripping my arm roughly as he pulls me into a sitting position. His voice is stern as he warns me, "I'll remove your gag. If you scream, I'll knock you out and not remove the gag again. Got it?" I nod silently, anger flickering in my eyes.

He removes the gag and puts the leather flask to my lips, and I drink as fast as possible before he yanks it away.

I requested food due to the pangs of hunger, and he offered me a few strips of jerky, which I devoured quickly. After finishing it, I dared to ask, "Why have you taken me?"

His response sends a shiver through me. "You've been accused of witchcraft and heresy. The Pope has ordered your capture for questioning." He repositions the gag tightly, cutting off any further questions.

He returns to his spot against a tree and settles down to sleep. I observe the surroundings —each man has an extra horse, allowing them to change horses to keep moving fast and rapidly. Suddenly, I hear the faint murmur of a river to the south, which is a potential clue to this location and a possible escape route.

I begin to plan my next move alone, surrounded by my thoughts and the daunting reality of my predicament. I know I must find a way to turn the tide in my favor before it's too late.

I try to reach out to Maynard and Finn through our mental connection. Maynard's reassuring voice responds, *"I'm tracking your path and updating Ashton and Finn on your location as I circle back."*

But there's silence from Finn; they're too far apart for my telepathic call to reach him. I resign myself to wait for the right moment to escape.

Within a few hours, the kidnappers abruptly haul me to my feet. One Jesuit busies himself with saddling the horses while the other uses his knife to cut the bindings around my feet. He gruffly informs me that if I need to relieve myself, now is the only opportunity until much later. One of them guides me to a secluded spot among the bushes; I seize the chance to relieve myself and decide it is now or never to enact my escape plan.

As I finish, stress rushes through my veins. This could be my only shot at freedom. I sprint toward the distant river, guided by the rushing water sounds. My agility serves me well as I leap over obstacles, narrowly dodging pursuit. I approach the riverbank and do not hesitate—I dive into the cold, rushing water with a splash that echoes behind me.

I feel relief, swiftly swimming downstream as I put distance between myself and my pursuers. The water helps loosen the leather straps around my wrists, and after pulling it firmly, I manage to free my hands. Now that I'm free, I push myself to swim even faster. A quick glance behind me reveals the Jesuit has almost caught up to me.

I take a deep breath and dive down as deep as possible, and I feel my strength increasing. My swimming is faster, and my lungs are not burning to air. Maybe adrenaline has kicked in? I'm not sure, but it was good timing to help me escape my captors.

Suddenly, a voice passes through my thoughts. It's Finn's voice, clear and urgent in her mind. *"Anwen, I can see you. Hide somewhere safe. We're coming for you."*

This mental connection with Finn is surprising, and I realize our bond has evolved in ways I never expected. I keep swimming, looking for a safe place to wait for Finn.

I spot a bend in the river with a flat, sandy area leading into the forest. Now that I need air, I decide to leave the water. As I surface, I gasp for breath, relieved to see the Jesuit falling behind. My feet touch the sand, and I jump out of the water, breaking into a sprint.

I start running through the forest, and my heart pounds. I dodge tree branches, leap over fallen logs, and use my hand to push away a limb blocking my path. Suddenly, I notice my hands are covered in white and bronze scales. "By the gods, what are those?" I think while still in shock.

I hear the pounding of hoofbeats coming straight at me—damn, the other Jesuit must have cut me off. I quickly vault to the side, but he jumps off his horse and collides with me in mid-air. I try to strike his windpipe but miss it, and they both are rolling to the ground to avoid getting hurt.

I scramble to my feet, only to be hit from behind by the other Jesuit. He clamps a foul-smelling rag over my nose and mouth as they struggle. I am losing the fight. The shock of seeing my hands covered in scales distracted me and cost me the escape. I continued to fight but could not win while being drugged. My strength fades, and I slip into unconsciousness.

The two Jesuits exchange a look. "Did you see her hands?" one of them asks. The other nods, "The devil works through her with wicked magic." Without wasting any time, they head back to their camp, gather the other horses, and continue their journey toward the Apostolic palace, where the Pope awaits them in Rome.

Ashton and Finn follow Maynard's directions to the abductors, but they cannot catch up. Suddenly, Finn stops and refuses to move. Ashton knows the horse has a reason for everything, so he dismounts. Finn looks him in the eye and then moves away. Ashton watches in amazement as the air shimmers and twirls around Finn, who begins to shapeshift into a dragon.

Finn shakes his large head, takes a few steps toward Ashton, and offers his front leg. Ashton is in awe of the magnificent creature, and he gently touches Finn's scales and says, "Very impressive, but I'm worried others will see us flying."

Finn shakes his head no and looks pointedly at his leg. Ashton realizes he needs to trust Finn and climbs onto the dragon's back.

Finn extends his massive wings with a few powerful steps and lifts off the ground. They soar straight up into the clouds, the wind rushing past them and the world below them disappearing from view.

Ashton quickly realizes they plan to hide among the clouds while following Maynard. He lets his mind wander. Father Thorne mentioned that the Pope knew Anwen's and Finn's extraordinary abilities during his recent visit. Their current direction of travel has them pointed to France, and he would bet then to Rome, Italy.

Ashton serves the Queen of England, which is hidden from everyone. His job is gathering intelligence on the Counter-Protestant Reformation within the Catholic Church. He is keenly aware of the Pope's biases against Spanish and Jewish communities and his harsh reforms of the Inquisition. The Pope's ambition to strengthen the

Roman Catholic Church's authority and suppress Protestantism and Judaism made him a formidable figure. Even his own Cardinals feared him.

Ashton sent a message to England's Queen through Banoff before leaving to warn her about the Pope's fabricated accusations of witchcraft against Anwen, Finn, and me. He has not disclosed Finn's and Anwen's abilities to the Queen yet because he knows he'll need allies in this dangerous situation. He could not be sure the Queen would want Anwen and Finn for England. It would be in all their best interests that the Queen only offer covert support at best.

In recent events shared with the Queen, the Pope issued a controversial decree targeting the Jewish community. He confines them to a Roman Ghetto, sealing them off from the city with a single gate that closes at sundown. The decree was brutal and cruel. This oppression provides a potential base for resistance—working together, they can liberate themselves and Anwen from the Pope's oppressive grip.

They make good progress, flying on Finn's back but trailing the abductors. Finn begins circling overhead, searching for a private spot to land safely and unseen. They find a clear area surrounded by trees and come down smoothly. Ashton dismounts, and Finn shifts back into his horse form, immediately grazing on the lush green grass nearby.

Shapeshifting and flying drain Finn's energy, so he needs to recharge by balancing between his forms. Meanwhile, Ashton gathers wood and skillfully starts a fire. He rummages through his bag for food rations, takes a refreshing sip from his water flask, and lays out his bedding for a brief nap.

As he goes into a light sleep, he finds himself in a dreamlike vision; a majestic dragon approaches him across a field of vibrant flowers. Its scales gleam white with bronze tips, catching the light with every graceful step. The dragon lowers its head, locking eyes with Ashton as if trying to convey a message.

Ashton reaches out tentatively, his hand brushing against the dragon's forehead and tracing down toward its snout. The creature holds his gaze; its presence is both powerful and serene. As the dragon slowly begins to fade away, Ashton feels a pang of longing, instinctively pleading for it to stay. He yearns deeply to keep this mystical being by his side.

Ashton awakens, shaken by the vivid dream of the dragon, pondering its significance. Finn is standing near to him and he speaks softly, "Finn, I dreamt of a magnificent dragon with white scales and bronze tips approaching me. It felt like it was trying to convey a message. This dream feels different and meaningful."

Finn nods in understanding. He remains in horse form as dawn breaks, needing rest from their flight. Ashton clears their campsite and prepares to continue their journey toward Rome. *Hang on, Anwen, we're coming.*

NINE

Facing Fears

I wake up in the dark. My eyes are slowly opening from the faint light coming through cracks in the ceiling. I feel cold stone pressed against my back and realize that I am being dragged down old stairs by my arms, somewhere deeper underground. I am frightened, but I force myself to remain quiet, keep my eyes closed, and listen to them intently. I hear obscure footsteps and whispers from far away. The air smells like dirt and something metallic, which sends a shiver down my spine. I try so hard to understand what they are murmuring, and it sounds like they are discussing a secret and dangerous plan. I know this is the start of a dreadful experience that all warriors face with trepidation and fear.

As I reach the bottom of the stairway, a suffocating darkness wraps around me. Dingy light barely filters through, creating dark and sinister shadows on the stone walls. I am feeling a heavy and depressing air like everyone around me is miserable and suffering. Every breath I take is full of bitterness and hopelessness. They drag me roughly along the cold and damp corridor, which is lined with cells on both sides.

The oppressive silence is shattered by an ear-piercing scream that echoes through the halls, a cry filled with such agony that it instills fear and a visceral, gut-wrenching response within my own body. At last, they stop at the final cell on the right. The heavy door creaks open, and they throw me on the cold and hard floor. And my body feels a painful thud that echoes through the room. The big metal door slammed shut behind me, and as soon they locked the door, the smells and remaining emotions in this cell assaulted me with fear and intense despair.

It takes all my strength to push myself off the ground, my body aching from the rough handling. I look around, and a filthy bucket is in the corner, and a dirty straw is scattered across the floor, giving off a musty smell. A bit of moonlight comes in from a small and narrow window high on the back wall, creating a ghostly glow. The walls on either side are rough, damp stone, and unwelcoming. I look across the corridor at the cell opposite mine, but it is empty, its shadows deep and ominous. The isolation feels heavy and suffocating as I realize just how alone I truly am.

I sit up straight, resting against the wall, and futilely try reaching out to Maynard, but *I can't*. For the first time in my life, I am truly alone and lost. I have trained for years as a rigorous warrior, which has honed my physical prowess. Nothing in life has prepared me for this total separation of mind and body from my friends. I realize I am terrified of what is ahead, and I pray to the gods that I will remain strong and courageous for what is to come. A loud door creaks open down the hall, drawing my attention. Two guards with their cruel faces, start dragging a prisoner toward the cell across from mine. They toss him in brutally and laugh about how he isn't so high and mighty now. The prisoner lies still. A slovenly, brutish guard exuding malice stops by my cell, his eyes narrowing as he sneers. "Look here, we've got a new one," he says menacingly. "I'll be enjoying breaking you in. I call first go at her."I don't rise to the guard's crude insinuations; it will only serve to fuel his lust to conquer and control me. I stare back at him, refusing to break eye contact, and then turn my back on him. His sneer deepens. "We'll see how brave you are soon enough."

The guard beside him chuckles but keeps his distance. "Don't go too hard on her, John," he says mockingly. "We want her to last a while."

The brutish guard laughs. "Oh, don't worry. I'll make sure she lasts." The other guard turns and walks away. John grabs the cell door and rattles it, raising his voice, "Look at me, you think you're so special? You're not now, are you?" Finally, he turns and slowly walks away. I will have to be close to death before he will touch me, for I will end his miserable life. I look across the aisle at the other prisoner, who has not moved. I decided it was time to start conserving my strength and slide down the stone wall to sit and rest.

A few hours later, food, better described as slop, is slid under my cell door in a beat-up tin dish. I hold my breath and force it down as fast as possible and barely prevent myself from retching. By the gods, but that was rank. The prisoner across the aisle is starting to move and groans. He drags himself over to his slop, quickly eats it all, and curls back up into a ball. I can now see his back is shredded through his shirt and still bleeding."My child," he says, his voice strained, "I'm sorry to see a woman here. I hope you have someone to pay your way out of this place."

"I don't," I reply bitterly. "I'm waiting for the Pope to grace me with his unholy presence."

He shakes his head in disbelief. "Ah, joy. The cruel, pompous Pope wants your company?"

"Yeah, something like that," I chuckle softly. "My name's Anwen. Who are you?"

"I am Cardinal Julius III from the seaport of Ancona," he introduces himself wearily. "It seems my presence as a Marrano Cardinal has angered the Pope, and now he wants to destroy me for apostasy. I fear he will succeed."

"I'm sorry to hear that," I say sincerely, "but don't lose hope. I have friends who will help us."

"We'll see," he replies, settling back. I decide it's best to try and rest, bracing myself for whatever is coming down that corridor next. When I wake up, the sun is peeking through the small window. I am desperate for the peace that nature brings my soul. I turn the refuse bucket over and climb up to the small window to look outside. There is a big beautiful oak tree near my window. The early morning sidelight dapples the grass, and I breathe deeply, calmly, and ask the gods to grace me with strength and honor.

It's been a restless night filled with fending off rats and keeping one eye open for that surly guard. I become tense as I hear the hallway door open, and I can only wait. The footsteps approach slowly. He stops at my cell and peers inside. He stands a bit taller than me, with brown hair, shifty brown eyes, and a thin-lipped mouth. He adorns himself with gold rings and necklaces and is dressed in the customary Pope attire of fine white and red linens.

"I hope you enjoyed your first night as my guest," he sneers. "It's just a taste of what's next to come. Anwen Elwen, you stand accused of heresy and witchcraft. The indictment is completed, and witness testimony has been gathered. Will you confess your sins?"

I narrow my eyes at him, standing defiantly with feet apart, arms behind my back, and straight shoulders. "You are a disgrace to your God, with your thirst for power and your slaughter of innocents," I declare firmly. "I confess to nothing."

The Pope's eyes narrow and light up. "Oh, I so hoped you'd say that. The interrogations will soon begin. I'm particularly curious about your horse dragon and how you summon dragon scales on your hands."

I carefully compose myself, keeping my expression neutral as I look into his eyes. "I have no idea what you're talking about. Those are nothing but fanciful tales. Dragons don't exist."

"We will uncover all your secrets," he persists. "I suspect you might be a Drakainas, gifted by the devil to carry out his will. It will be intriguing to see if we can provoke a transformation; torture allows no room for concealment."

He turns to the guard and instructs him to have me stripped by the Inquisitor in search of any devil's mark. The guard smirks, but the Pope interrupts. "Do not touch her with your sinful ways. Is that clear?" The guard nods humbly. "Yes, Your Holiness."

The Pope smiles at me, turns, and slowly walks away.

My hands and feet are shackled, and I can only take small steps as I am escorted to a room off the main hallway. I am left standing alone in the center, and I note the various collections of tools for torture.

Suddenly, a giant man enters wearing only leggings and boots. His wrists are wrapped in leather cuffs, and his lips curl in an evil smirk. He seizes a knife from a nearby table without any word and methodically cuts away all my clothes, even my boots. I stand before him, vulnerable and naked, as he inspects every inch of my body. His inspection suddenly stops when he sees something on my right inner arm. He grabs my arm, turns it over, and declares proudly, "There it is the devil's mark!"

I expected to see a mole but was shocked to find a small bronze-colored dragon-shaped head. "God, when did that appear?" I turn to watch the guard. He ignores me, grabs an oversized, coarse brown tunic, throws it at me, seizes my arm, and roughly pushes me out the door. I cover myself with the tunic as best as I can, but my back is still visible as I walk back down the hallway to my cell. The guard opens the door, shoves me inside, unlocks my shackles, and whispers, "See you soon," before locking the cell door behind him.

I quickly wrap the rough cloth around myself, still feeling vulnerable despite its decent coverage. The fabric falls down to my mid-shins, and I start to shiver in fear. How and will I be able to endure more torture? To focus my mind and tuck fear away before it overwhelms me, I drop to the ground, start exercising to keep my physical health strong, and soon lose myself in the repetitive movements. I think about the sudden appearance of the dragon head on my arm and the strange scales on my hands. The Pope's suggestion that I might be a Drakainas—a mythical creature with a woman's upper body and a serpent's tail—uh, no thanks.

Something inside me is changing, transforming me in ways I don't understand. Well, my life is a shit show anyway, so might as well add more to it.

They serve a single meal per day, and as the food arrives each day, I eat quickly and watch my cellmate across the hall. He is moving slowly, appearing frail, and his complexion is grey. Even conversation seems to be too much for him now, so I stay quiet. I try to contact Maynard again, but I do not receive any response. I lean against the wall and think about my situation. I had thought I would be mentally stronger than this, *but I felt shattered.*

TEN

Hang On Anwen

I am imprisoned, and I can't find a way out. I am holding on *just* because I have the slightest hope that my friends will rescue me in time...

Ashton rides Finn through the Roman Ghetto gate as sundown is fast approaching. The gate is an imposing structure of weathered stone that is ready to close the city off for the night. The people move like shadows themselves, hunched shoulders, eyes downcast, quickly moving out of the way. It is painfully obvious how they are mistreated, and their hope has been crushed by oppression. Ashton finds the stable and dismounts. He asks for a place for Finn to stay, some bedding, and food. The stable master is a rough-looking man who's actually kind-hearted and arranges everything right away. Finn soon settles in for the night and munching on fresh hay.

Ashton watches Maynard swoop down and land briefly on Finn's saddle before flying off again into the darkening sky. He hopes that Maynard is searching for my whereabouts. Ashton has a strong suspicion that the Pope is holding her, but the question is where? The thought makes him uneasy. He knew Anwen could take care of herself, but they were against much larger numbers now, a mighty enemy that didn't hesitate to murder people for the slightest infractions. Maynard got them this far. Hopefully, she would be able to narrow down their search. He couldn't lose her; he just found his true mate. He feels a knot of fear tighten in his chest. He is furious enough to tear the city apart brick by brick and fueled by desperation. But he knows he needs to stay calm, to think clearly if he is going to save me.

After ensuring Finn is comfortable for the night, Ashton makes his way to the Piping Kettle Inn. The inn is warm and lively, with candles softly illuminating the interior and groups of people murmuring in low voices. The scent of stew fills the air, making him hungry. He walks in, feeling the weight of the day pressing down on him, but he pushes it aside. He needs to gather his strength to rest and plan his next move.

Ashton finds comfort at a small table tucked against the back wall. He orders a hearty meal and secures a room for the next two nights; his mind is still racing with thoughts about me and the dangerous situation they all are now entangled in.

While he was waiting, he overheard the conversations around him. People are talking about the Pope's new rules, whispers of disagreements, and strange events. One old man, leaning over his drink, mentions a secret tunnel under the city that leads to the Pope's quarters. He tucks this information away for later to investigate.

He is waiting for his food while his eyes scan the room, and he notices a particular person quietly sipping a drink in the far corner. His meal arrives, and he quickly locks eyes with the mysterious patron across the room before heading upstairs. He goes up the stairs, finds his room, and steps inside. It's modestly furnished with a single bed, a nightstand, a chamber pot, and a washstand. He hears a knock at his door, three quick knocks, a pause, and then two more. He opens the door to let the man from downstairs into his room.

Thomas stands before him, an experienced spy working for the Queen of England. It is no coincidence that their paths have crossed in Rome at such a critical time. They firmly shake hands, understanding the seriousness of the ongoing circumstances. Ashton offers him a chair and immediately starts asking Thomas questions.

"Good to see you again, friend," Ashton begins. "Have you discovered anything?"

Thomas nods solemnly, "Indeed, I have. A young woman is accused of heresy, and witchcraft is brought to the Pope's dungeons a few days ago by the Jesuits. Her description matches Anwen's. The Pope has personally arranged everything and handles the interrogations himself; she will be subjected to torture till she confesses she is a witch and then publicly executed." Ashton leans back, looking tired, as he runs a hand through his messy hair. "How well-guarded is the dungeon, and do we have detailed maps of its layout?" he asks urgently.

Thomas sighs, "We have some maps," he says carefully. "The dungeon has many guards. Sneaking in and out won't be easy; we'll need a distraction." He pauses, sounding regretful. "I'm sorry, Ashton. The Queen can't send more help than this reconnaissance. But I'll be there with you as a friend."

Ashton nods seriously, gratitude in his eyes. "Thank you, Thomas. Your support means a lot."

They plan to meet again with the maps and finalize their goal. After a firm handshake, Thomas wishes him goodnight and leaves Ashton to his thoughts.

He burns with anger, but he sets it aside and concentrates on the task at hand—*rescuing me before it is too late*. He gets ready for bed, but he is unable to sleep easily. Tossing and turning, he drifts into a restless dream. He finds himself in a surreal landscape of swirling white smoke where reality merges with fantasy. I am standing beside a magnificent dragon, its scales shimmering in white and bronze shade. I touch the dragon's neck gently with some sort of understanding. Suddenly, we submerge underwater, gliding effortlessly through an unknown world. Ashton wakes up, and his heart is racing. What do these vivid dreams mean? Are they just his fears, or do they have a deeper message for him? He thinks about the images and feels a strong and urgent connection. Something inside him stirs, urging him to follow and understand the dream's message. He made a firm decision to put his worries aside to find answers and rescue me while being aware that time was *running out.*

ELEVEN

Courage and Pain

Another dark day starts, and I am being held for sins I never committed.

I gasp for air, sputtering water from my nose and mouth. I'm pushed back into the cold water and held under until my lungs feel like they're going to burst. I can't hold my breath any longer, and I involuntarily swallow water, feeling it burn as it fills my lungs. I'm yanked up roughly, and through my fear and pain, I hear the Inquisitor's voice saying, "Confess your sins of witchcraft and heresy!"

I'm too desperate for air to respond; my chest is heaving, and my vision is blurry. I'm plunged underwater again, the pressure on my chest growing so unbearable that I almost black out. I'm pulled up once more, and my body is weak and unresponsive. My hands are tied tightly behind my back, and my feet are dangling off the floor, leaving me completely powerless against the relentless torture.

I hear a calm female voice while I'm dunked underwater, *"Just breathe, Anwen. Don't fight it."*

Panic surges through me. I know I'm dying, and the voice must be a hallucination from the lack of oxygen. But I can't resist the urge anymore. I am inhaling deeply, and the water is flooding my lungs. Pain shoots through me, but then inexplicably, my lungs relax, and I can suddenly breathe. I'm dragged up again and then shoved back underwater, and my mind is spinning from the surreal experience of finding air in the water.

The soothing female voice speaks again, *"I am Lyra, your dragon; our souls are intertwined, and we are one."* I'm pulled up again, but this time, I find myself staring into the eyes of the Pope. I retch up the water in my lungs.

His eyes widen as he notices small scales on one side of my lower jaw. "Call the dragon forth now, do it!" he commands.

I smile defiantly, "There you go again, talking about dragons like they are real."

He slaps me hard across the face and speaks urgently to the Inquisitor. Despite the pain, this moment feels oddly satisfying, and it's worth all the pain.

The Inquisitor roughly spins me around, strips off my gown, and lays me on a cold and hard table. He pulls my arms above my head and secures them along with my feet to the table before leaving the room.

The Pope circles around me with his eyes fixed on the dragon mark on my skin. He touches my mark with wide eyes, "I will make you shift. Why fight it?"

I laugh, "You're nuts, you know that?" The absurdity of the situation emits my fear, but when I laugh, it shows resistance against the madness happening around me.

The Pope laughs cruelly, grabbing my nipple and twisting it hard. Tears fill my eyes, but I stay silent. He releases me and starts slapping my face repeatedly. He says with a threatening voice, "You won't be laughing for long. I am not interested in you sexually. I only want your dragon. I want to control it. You will call it forth and make it obey me."

He turns me over, grabs a leather strap, and slaps it against his - hand menacingly while commanding me to shift.

I am quiet, and the first hit lands across my back, followed by more. I bite my tongue to not scream, but the relentless beating keeps going. My back feels like it's on fire, my breaths coming in short, ragged gulps, and I'm panting as I'm covered in a cold sweat while struggling to bear the intense pain. Suddenly, the female voice in my head speaks, "I can heal you later, but I will take some of the pain for you now."

I notice the pain is easing, though he is continuously hitting me, and I feel a renewed strength to survive the ordeal. The beating goes on, but now I believe that I can withstand it. I share my gratitude with my dragon, "He can break my body, but he will never claim my spirit, for I now have a dragon's heart, and it beats for freedom." I feel my dragon's embrace around the light of my soul.

Finally, the Pope stops because he is drenched in sweat and his face is red. He wipes his face with a cloth, leans in close to me, and sneers, "We will resume your interrogation tomorrow. Till then, enjoy trying to lie down tonight."

I say, "I may bleed, but I am unbroken. For every scar you leave, I grow stronger, like iron in the forge."

He turns away, and the door opens as the Inquisitor returns. He unshackles me from the table, picks me up, grabs my gown, throws me over his shoulder, and carries me back to my cell. He drops me randomly, tosses my gown at me, and leaves after locking the cell door behind him.

I am trembling as I grip the bars for support. I pull on my gown, and it sticks immediately to my bleeding back, making me hiss in pain. Then, I ask Lyra through my mind, *"Are you okay?"*

She responds with a soft snort, *"You are worried for me, and yet you were tortured."*

"What are you?" I ask.

"I am you, and you are me - we are as one. You were called a dragon shifter in my time. I am a water dragon that you have called from within yourself. I need to heal some of your wounds. Try and rest." Lyra replies.

I feel warmth spreading across my back, and the pain begins to subside considerably. *"Thank you,"* I say, *"I wouldn't have made it out alive today without your help."*

"You are welcome. We have to rest now." Lyra says.

I lie on the dirty straw, settling on my stomach, and fall into a fitful sleep. My body is aching, but my spirit is bolstered by the presence of the dragon inside me.

I wake up as cold water splashes over me, which is thrown by the Inquisitor. He unlocks the cell, shackles me, and leads me back to the torture room. My heart is racing, and my body is trembling uncontrollably. The Pope is waiting for me as I enter, and his eyes are cold and calculating. He starts inspecting me with a critical eye, then whispers something to the Inquisitor, who grabs a knife from the table and cuts away my gown. The fabric tears away with a painful rip, reopening wounds and causing me to stifle a cry. Blood begins to trickle down my back again. I'm chained to a line that descends from the ceiling and ends in a hook that clasps onto my handcuffs. My arms are forced upwards, and the chain tightens until my toes barely touch the floor. The Inquisitor leaves me alone in the ominous room.

The Pope circles me and stops in front of me, gripping my jaw tightly to force me to look at him. "You think you can still defy me, you heretic witch?" he smirks.

I boldly spit on his face and smiled, "There's your answer."

He wipes the spittle from his face with his sleeve and strikes me across the cheek with a backhand. I cannot see out of one eye due to the swelling, and both sides of my lips are split and bleeding; my nose has a continuous trickle of blood.

"I think I need to wash my face. I'll return later for our conversation," he says slowly as he exits the room.

I strain on my tiptoes, trying to alleviate some of the weight on my arms. This is today's torture. The Inquisitor enters, placing kindling and wood into the fireplace. Iron rods are added as the fire crackles and make shadows bounce across the room. He then sharpens his knives thoroughly before leaving without a word. I lose track of time hanging there in the oppressive heat, and my dragon is also silent. Suddenly, the Pope returns, but he is no longer in his formal robes and dressed simply in a brown robe. As he passes me toward the fireplace, he spits in my face.

I can't help but laugh rebelliously, "Feel better?"

The Pope pauses by the fireplace and puts a large glove on before selecting a red-hot iron rod adorned with the symbol 'W' at its tip. He holds it dangerously close to my eye and threatens, "Today, you will summon your dragon and be marked as a witch."

I choose silence and brace myself. The Pope moves behind me, grabs my hair to wrench my head back, and then drives the rod into my right shoulder blade. I explode through pain and screams and struggle against his grip as he cruelly laughs. He retrieves the rod and returns it to the flames with a chilling promise, "Today, 'W' will be branded all over you. If you still refuse to call your dragon, then I have far worse methods."

I whisper through my agony, "What's wrong with you? How can you do these things and call yourself a holy man?"

He declares, "I am a devout Catholic. I will not allow other religions, kings, queens, or immigrants with their Marrano beliefs to undermine our church and beliefs. I will use any means necessary to eradicate those who threaten our religion. I despise women; they are the weakest gender and easily get manipulated by the Devil for his ends, and you are a prime example of that. I have studied dragons and magic and know their potential, but you are the first I have witnessed attempting transformation. Once I control the dragon, it will simply exert complete dominance and enforce the will of the church. The Inquisition will persist, and fear will maintain order."

He turns toward the wall to reclaim a leather strap and begins to slap it against his palm. I roll my eyes and say, "You do enjoy theatrics, don't you?" While I am desperately calling out to the dragon inside me for help, there is no response. My body shivers tensely, my breathing and heart rate expedite, and I sweat amply, but I still feel chilled.

He declares exasperatedly, "I am tired of this game now! Summon your dragon."

Suddenly, I come to the realization I am going to die in this miserable place today, and my soul calms with acceptance and grace. I say, "No matter the chains, no matter the pain, I will never betray the fire in my soul."

I close my eyes as the strap goes back and forth until, thankfully, *I pass out*.

TWELVE

Dances with Shadows

Night presses down like a heavy shroud over the castle walls.

Ashton is struggling to sleep well at night and barely getting rest. In the morning, he quickly breaks his fast and is keen to start their plan of finding me. He also makes sure Finn is taken care of and informs him of the final plan before he deals with his other tasks. Finn and Maynard have repeatedly attempted to mind speak with Anwen but could not get her to respond. Finn is in a vengeful state of mind and shares with Maynard that men will pay for abducting and harming Anwen. He will burn them alive today.

Thomas meets Ashton at the stable, and they both go to his room to start planning *my rescue*. Thomas's detailed maps prove invaluable as they uncover that the dungeon is located beneath a papal tower with a single entrance and exit. Inside the tower, there are two corridors, each leading to the left and the right. Each corridor has four cells on either side, making a total of eight cells per corridor. There is also a large room off to the side, which Ashton guesses is the 'torture chamber.'

The mere thought of what I might be enduring makes his stomach simmer with nausea. He suddenly feels an overwhelming sadness or resignation. He pushes his thoughts down that single fragile tether in his mind, "In the darkest of battles, I found you- my light, my reason to fight. Fight for us, Anwen, don't give up, my heart." Their planning is complete, and now, it's time to act.

Thomas obtains second-hand clothing and a distinctive yellow hat from his contacts so he can look like 'Marrano.' Meanwhile, Ashton dresses in simple dark attire with a plain shirt and pants tucked into his boots. He loosely attaches handcuffs to Thomas's wrists but does not secure them. Near the tower, a crowd gathers. They are armed with torches and pitchforks and demanding the release of their imprisoned family members. The clamor grows louder as more people join the protest. This action caused guards from the papal tower to come out and control the expanding crowd.

Ashton takes advantage of the planned distraction to sneak into the tower. He takes the lead and urges Thomas to go forward toward the entrance of the tower. They slip inside without alerting the guards as Ashton guides him down the right corridor. He looks inside each cell to find me. They turn back and retrace their steps to the opposite corridor and begin their search when a guard intercepts them. He starts to question them about their purpose for being in the tower. Ashton claims that they are given a task by the Pope to transfer a prisoner to their cell.

The guard stares at them before agreeing, "We have an empty cell. A prisoner passed away last night. You can use that one."

Thomas glances at Ashton and notes his eyes are bright red, almost glowing, and his body vibrates with rage.

The guard takes the keys out from his waistband and leads the way to them. As they approach the last cell, the guard unlocks the door, and Ashton decisively seizes the guard's head between his hands and snaps his neck. They drag the guard into the cell and lock the cell door. As Ashton looks up across him, his heart breaks at the sight of a woman lying motionless and face down in the cell. He recognizes that it's me and growls in anger and fear. He snatches the keys and runs to unlock the door. As he opens the door, he finds me in a grievous state and struggles to hold back his scream of fury at the indignity that happened to me. He gently brushes my hair aside and whispers for me to hang on. He lifts me carefully into his arms.

He tells Thomas with sadness in his eyes, "Let's get her out of this place."

Thomas nods firmly, discards his hat, and draws a hidden sword from his trousers. He leads the way to the exit, and Ashton runs up the stairs while holding me. Just as we reach the top, the Inquisitor steps out from the torture room and shouts at us, "Stop!"

They both ignore him and break through the exit. Ashton immediately whistles for Finn and waits for the dragon to show up. The Inquisitor is roaring behind them and orders the guards to stop us. Thomas engages the guards who are coming near and tells Ashton to flee, "Hurry up, get out of here!"

All eyes turn skyward as darkness falls upon them. The sun is obscured, and a massive shadow descends with a deafening roar, landing heavily enough to shake the ground. Finn pivots toward the guards, and unleashes a torrent of fire that engulfs everyone closest to him and reduces them instantly to ash. Panic sweeps through the mob and drives them to scatter in terror. The Inquisitor is standing resolute and observes Ashton as he gets on Finn, and Thomas carefully passes me into his arms. He joins them on the dragon's back, and with a powerful thrust from Finn's legs, we ascend into the air.

Ashton is holding me closer, his tears falling on bruises on my face, and it makes him furious about the pain I have endured. "How can I keep you safe when your spirit is as fierce as the fight itself?" He feels guilty for failing to protect me and silently pleads with God, "Please, spare her life. I beg you." There is no answer, just the steady, intense sounds of the wind rushing over dragon wings.

Finn selects a spot to rest and finds refuge under a suitable tree cover near a large lake. Finn finds me still unconscious as he attempts to communicate through mind-speaking while Maynard circles overhead and cries out in distress. Finn feels Ashton's heartbreak over their friend's suffering. Men can be monsters sometimes, but he promises to make things right by seeking justice. We dismount, and he shifts his shape and immediately starts eating grass. Maynard alights briefly on a tree branch before taking a flight to keep watch for potential attackers. Thomas sets up a minimal campsite while Ashton slings a leather bag over his shoulder and carries me to the lakeside to cleanse my wounds.

He carefully removes my clothes and is shocked after looking at my injuries. His body is shaking with anger and sorrow. He starts cleansing my wounds and is relieved that I'm still unconscious and not feeling the pain. Ashton cares for me and realizes he must let me return to my own timeline and realm. Using Rune Magic, he can summon a portal that will transport us back to our timeline. He kept his ability to control opening and closing portals a secret from me, for he wanted time to win my affection, and he hoped that I would fall in love with him as deeply as he did from the moment he first saw me. He knew from my first snarky comments and display of courage that I would be his. He knows now that *his selfish desire to win my love nearly cost my life.*

He can't protect me from the Pope's army of Jesuits and their political power. Once I am safely away, he vows to destroy the Pope and everything he represents. The Pope is a monster that needs to be eradicated for my sake and the good of humanity as well.

I become aware I am in a safe, comforting place free from pain and fear, where I can peacefully drift. It is so calm and comforting that I don't want to leave.

Suddenly, Lyra's voice reached out to me, expressing regret. *"I could not help you more. My powers are weakened without shifting in water, and that is where I gain strength and abilities. I am so sorry Anwen."*

I still find ease in her soothing words and feel a deep and soulful connection. I reassured her, *"Don't worry, my friend. Without the help you gave me, I would not have survived. You gave me hope – such a powerful emotion that even evil could not crush my spirit. You saved my soul."* She drifted back into the dark oblivion of quiet peace. Her dragon spirit curled around the light that was Anwen, cocooning her in her love and healing. Her brave little human.

THIRTEEN

Planning Revenge

I wake up in a stunning canopied bed, the light green silk curtains softly swaying as sunlight streams through the arched windows with a warm glow of light at the foot of the bed. I stretch my limbs and wince as a sharp pain reminds me of the Pope's torture. I panic as I bolt upright, my eyes roaming around the room in search of any danger. My heart pounds in my chest, and each beat echoes like a drum.

I see a large, dark-haired warrior slumped in a chair beside my bed, and his rhythmic snores buzz in the room. Despite his formidable appearance, I smile, so he isn't perfect after all. I cherish this private insight. This male risked everything to rescue me from a certain horrendous death. He is such an honorable male. My heart swells with love, and I now understand the meaning of "love conquers all," for I have now surrendered my entire self to my mate.

I attempt to swing my legs to the side of the bed, but the pain is so intense that I can't help but gasp. In an instant, he is out of the chair and by my side. He leans in close with his face just inches away from mine, studying my features intently before he stares at my eyes. Gently, he presses his lips to mine. The tenderness in his touch overwhelms me, and tears begin to spill down my cheeks.

Smiling through my tears, I whisper, "I have missed you, Dark Hair."

He responds with his characteristic side smirk, "I missed you more."

His smirk vanishes, and his eyes drop in sorrow. "I'm so sorry I failed to protect you, my mate." He said, his voice choked with guilt. "I know how much you've suffered from your wounds. Those who caused this pain will pay for it, I promise."

His words are heavy with remorse. I reach out to him with my hand gently touching his cheek, lifting his face to look into mine. "You don't need to blame yourself," I say softly. "It's your love that makes me unbreakable. I've faced my fears and endured the pain and loneliness. We will defeat the Pope and the Inquisitor, putting an end to their cruelty, freeing women and men of their evil tyranny and abuse."

He nods as he gently helps me get out of bed and guides me to a nearby chair and table. "I have some food prepared and brought up for us," he says with a reassuring smile. "Let me set it on the table.

As he leaves the room to bring the food, I settle into the chair peacefully. Suddenly, Lyra's voice echoes in my mind which is playful and curious, *"My, oh my! He's quite the gallant knight. And he's your mate?"*

I smile warmly with a soft glow of affection in my eyes and say, "Yes, he is my mate. I have accepted him, and I love him deeply."

While I am admitting to my feelings, Ashton walks into the room with food and hears everything. He pauses as intense emotions wash over him. He closes his eyes for a moment and savors the profound joy of knowing I have accepted him as my mate and love him so deeply. The weight of his duty presses heavily on him now. He knows that to fully hold on to our bond and secure our future together, he has to eliminate the threats that loom over our lives. His resolve grows stronger; he is determined to protect our love and make our relationship complete.

Ashton and I are enjoying our breakfast together, with me recounting the harrowing events from the Inquisitor's torture chamber and any fragments of information I can recall. After I finish eating, Ashton carefully lifts me and places me back in bed with tender care.

"Rest, little one," he says softly, his voice filled with warmth and determination. "I need to start making plans, but I'll return to you as soon as I can."

With his reassuring words and the comfort of his presence, I begin to drift off to sleep almost immediately as my exhaustion pulls me toward a deep, healing sleep. Ashton goes to meet Thomas in his study room, where his old friend greets him with a serious expression. Thomas relays urgent news that he needs to report to the Queen immediately. There is recent intel that the King of France has been meeting with the Pope concerning the Knights Templar. The King of France and the Pope are now branding the Knights Templar as a dangerous threat, and Ashton can already see where this is headed. The Knights Templar have devoted everything to their religious convictions and accumulated substantial wealth and land over time— wealth that the Pope and King now greedily covet. The King of France and the Pope also fear its power and military strength.

Witnesses have been found at the papal tower, and they have seen Finn's dragon, but they agree to deny that the event ever occurred. Thomas ensured palms were laden with coins to prevent the locals from supporting the Pope's insane claims of a dragon killing his guards.

Ashton hopes that Thomas can persuade the Queen of England to either officially distance herself from the conflict or discreetly provide additional support for the impending struggle against the corrupt forces within the church. He is certain that divine justice is not on the side of the church's abuses and wrongdoing.

"I'll keep you updated on any changes," Thomas says in a steady voice. "Give my regards to your lady." With that, he steps out of the castle, mounts his horse, and rides off toward London.

Some moments later, Ashton meets with Banoff for a briefing on the latest developments. He shares the troubling news and outlines his plan to take me back to my home once I am recovered enough to travel. He requests Banoff prepare and charge the rune magic needed to open and close the portal.

They are also discussing strategies to remove the Pope and Inquisitor from power, weighing various methods and potential consequences.

Banoff is aware of individuals who oppose the corrupt church and plans to enlist them to challenge its authority. He is focusing on organizing these allies and setting the plan into motion, while Ashton needs to prepare me for my return back home with my friends.

Ashton will escort me to House Elwen, where he will inform my father about the perils we have faced and his strategy to dismantle those responsible for the suffering. Ashton will provide as many of his warriors as possible, but he will need more. Hopefully, he can persuade

Anwen's father to temporarily provide additional Elven warriors for the upcoming battle with the Pope's army.

However, he knows the fight against the church's power is a risk, and he might not prevail on his own. He is comfortable with the fact that he has other allies who have similar goals.

Ashton imparts the importance of keeping their plans a secret. If other Houses or Churches gained knowledge of their plans, it would jeopardize their chances of winning this battle. Banoff says, "Understood," and takes his leave to begin implementing their plan.

Meanwhile, Ashton conducts a thorough inspection of the castle, both inside and outside, to ensure its security. The drawbridge is raised, and guards are posted along the upper wall walkways, diligently scanning for any signs of intruders on his land. It is only after he is satisfied with these security measures that he feels it is safe to return to *me*.

FOURTEEN

Cookies and Kisses

Ashton steps into the busy kitchen, and it smells really good because something yummy is baking. He approaches the head cook to request the sweetest cookies for me. The cook's eyes sparkle with a smile on her face as she carefully retrieves a batch of golden oatmeal and raisin cookies from the oven. As she arranges the cookies on a delicate plate, a young kitchen maid is busy brewing a pot of fragrant tea, and the steam looks like little clouds. Ashton thanks them with gratitude as he carries the plate and teapot to his beloved. He knows the conversation awaiting him with me will not be easy, but he hopes the thoughtful treats will soften the moment because he knows that my love of sweets easily sways my heart.

I am sitting in my favorite chair by the open window, looking outside. The wind is softly blowing in through the window. It smells like fresh grass and flowers. The sounds of birds chirping and the leaves rustling are the serene sounds of nature's beauty, making my soul calm and relaxed.

The nap I have taken has restored me and made me feel more like myself physically. Despite the peace around me, my inner peace is fragile. Memories of the time in the papal tower invade my thoughts with relentless persistence. These flashbacks surge through me like a tidal wave, dragging me back to the dark moments I desperately wish to escape. I am panicked, and it's causing my heart to race uncontrollably. The cold sweat and rapid breaths are relentless, like a storm I can't weather. Sometimes, I feel as though I am trapped in my mind, reliving the horrors over and over, unable to find calm.

It isn't healthy for me to sit idly and wait for disturbing memories to bombard and immobilize me. I am a creature of action. Every warrior has two fears: the possibility of being maimed or tortured, and I am different now. I can bear both visible and hidden scars, yet I face my deepest fear of capture and torment head-on. Through my trials, I discover my limits and surpass my fears. The pure light within my soul remains with me, and Lyra's support provides me the strength to endure it all.

My body is healing effectively, thanks to the powers of my water dragon. I feel a deep gratitude for the dragon, though I am still confused about our bond. I asked Finn about it, and he explained that he had used a few drops of his blood to stop me from bleeding out when the portal transported us. And he suggests that this may have triggered a genetic response within me. Finn continues to express his desire to see me "in the flesh" and I have promised that I will visit soon.

During the day, I keep the window open so Maynard can fly in and visit me. I find myself having to continuously reassure Ashton and my friends that they are not to blame for what happened to me; instead, it is the Pope's wrongdoing—I can see their persistent guilt. It hurts me to see them suffer from such emotions, and I know they are carrying a burden that is not theirs to bear.

A sudden knock on the door pulls me from my thoughts. "Enter," I say with a soft voice. Ashton steps in carefully, carrying a tray laden with cookies and tea. The enticing aroma of freshly baked cookies causes my eyes to sparkle with delight. I smile warmly and pat the seat beside me. Ashton places the tray on the table next to me and sits on the chair. He hands me a napkin and pours the tea. He leans back to look at me with dreamy eyes. I quickly reach for the cookies, savoring their warmth and gooey sweetness—just the way I love them.

I roll my eyes and moan playfully, causing him to shift into his chair. The moan reminds him of cherished memories of our intimate moments. I continue to savor the cookies; my enjoyment is evident. "If you want a cookie, you'd better grab one quickly," I tease him.

He smiles as he picks up a cookie. He licks the edge while watching me intently, then delicately nibbles the cookie's edge. I find myself mesmerized by the way he savors the treat. "By the Gods, I never knew I wanted to be a cookie!" He playfully places the cookie between his teeth, running his tongue over and under it before taking a slow, deliberate bite. The sight is both enchanting and tempting. I shifted in my chair as I couldn't take my eyes away from him. He bites a tiny piece and sucks it into his mouth. Even something as mundane as eating a cookie charges me with intimacy and desire. He sets the cookie aside and picks up the teacup, swirling his finger in the warm liquid before tasting it and smiling. The room feels warm suddenly; I start fanning myself with my napkin and smile back at him.

He whispers, "I love you, Anwen. You are my mate for life."

I lower my eyes and start playing with my napkin. Though I am a warrior, he has managed to dismantle my defenses and uncover a softer and more vulnerable side of me. His love leaves me feeling both deeply desired and more connected than ever.

Ashton looks at me with concern and asks, "How is your healing coming along?"

"The water dragon is aiding my recovery, and while I have no open wounds left, I still feel sore and bruising." I reply, "I need to start exercising soon to regain my strength."

He nods thoughtfully, "I need to speak to you about a few things if you're up to it." His tone is serious, and I am worried.

What could be so urgent? He reaches for my hand, gently drawing circles on my palm as he begins to speak.

"I have a magical ability I haven't shared with you yet," he confesses. "I can open and close portals with the help of runes. I didn't tell you before because I wanted to win your love first. I realize now how selfish and dangerous that was."

I am surprised and confused. He continues, "I must remove the Pope and Inquisitor from power, but I can't protect you from his army of Jesuits and their influence. I need you to be safe while I complete this mission. I want to take you back to your home, meet your father, and share my plans. Will you stay in your home realm until I can finish this?"

As Ashton shares his plan, a torrent of emotions surges through me. I feel anger that he doubts my combat abilities, fear for his safety, and anxiety about him being in my land where half-breeds face execution. The thought of him being captured, hurt, or killed gnaws at me.

Ashton is still silent, gently circling his fingers on my palm as he watches me intently. I am unable to contain my turmoil, so I pull my hand away, stand up, and walk to the window. I stand tall, shoulders squared, and hands clasped behind my back. Turning to face him, I let him see the raw emotions etched on my face—anger, fear, and deep concern. He stands and walks toward me, gently cradling my face in his hand. Tears begin to spill from my eyes, frustrating me, for I can't control it, and it pisses me off.

I turn away, looking out the window with an emotional voice. "Do what you know is right, but I cannot guarantee that when I am physically able to join this fight against this unholy evil, I will stay away."

Ashton knows he has wounded my pride, but his need to protect me outweighs everything else. The sight of my tears and the pain in my voice cuts him deeply, but his love for me makes the thought of me in danger unbearable.

I sigh with a weary voice. "I am tired; perhaps it is time you leave."

Ashton's eyes widen, then narrow, "I don't think so, little one. There will be no resentment or anger between us; we must work together to see this through."

Before I can respond, I feel his breath on my neck, then a tender lick and the gentle suction of his lips. I close my eyes and indulge. It feels so good; I trust this man with my body and soul. He continues to lick my neck slowly, moving around to my earlobe, and whispers, "You are special to me; I would not survive losing you, Anwen."

His hand lightly brushes my nipple, and I sigh with a soft moan. "I don't want to frighten you after your captivity," he says gently. "You must be honest and tell me to stop, and I will."

I don't want him to stop. In his arms, I can forget everything but him. I turn, grab his head, and pull him down for a hard and passionate kiss. He presses his hips against my dress, right where my desire aches for him, and it feels incredibly good. His mouth and tongue move to tease my nipple to a peak, then shift to the other breast, licking that nipple, sending shock waves to my core. I push my hips against him, seeking the release only he can provide.

He does it all so well, and I cherish how he skillfully stimulates both my mind and my body with a potent combination that leaves me breathless. He moves his hips with intensity as he slides up and down my sex, pushing me toward the edge of pleasure. "Don't stop, Ashton," I demand with a voice desperate with desire.

He responds with a low moan, gently pressing me against the wall, his hands bracketing my head. He becomes faster, driving me to a shattering climax. As I cry out, clutching his shoulders and feeling my legs weaken. He doesn't slow down, his breath coming in heavy pants as he moves rhythmically. By the gods, it feels like I am on the edge of releasing once more, climbing toward the peak with each powerful thrust. In a deep raspy whisper against my ear, he says, "Come for me again, now." I do, as I call out his name. All I know is he makes me want him over and over.

He tilts his head back and lets out a low, throaty moan as he hits the height of his pleasure. He slows down and tenderly kisses me slowly and affectionately. He says with a half-smile, "We'll consummate our mating when these dangers are behind us, and you can declare your love for me over and over."

I laugh softly, "Smug male."

He grins, "Yes, I am, where you are concerned."

And then, as I watch him walk away, the sight of his strong, long legs and firm backside makes me wish I could run my hands over him.

"When we finally become mated, there better be a bunch of cookies near to keep my stamina up!"

I smile as I hear his laughter as he walks down the hallway.

FIFTEEN

A Battle in Two Realms

I am working tirelessly to rebuild my strength, fiercely determined to reclaim my health as rapidly as possible. I decide to leave the castle for the first time and visit Finn. As I approached the stable, Finn was galloping in the pasture toward me. He made a sliding stop and dropped his head to my chest, and his soft muzzle nibbled on my hand. We mind-speak, and I said, *"I missed you, ole man."*

He lifts his head with a curious sniff and asks, *"You smell different. Is it the water dragon?"*

I smile with relief and warmth, *"Yes, her name is Lyra. She's my healer and guardian, doing everything she can to aid me. Her presence is a comfort, though sometimes her shimmering scales appear on my face or hands when I'm under stress. She is as beautiful as she is kind. Despite being a dragon, she doesn't possess the fierce demeanor one might expect from a warrior."*

Finn's ears prick forward, and he tilts his head inquisitively to the side, *"I need to shift and see if I can mind speak with her; she isn't responding to me in our current forms."*

I nod with a concerned etch on my face, *"She needs water to strengthen herself, and she hasn't shifted yet."*

Finn's expression grows more serious as he lifts his head, *"That's alarming! She has to shift. We must help her."*

I feel a bit anxious because I know he's right, but I'm not sure how to assist her other than immersing her in water. Finn and I decided to try the next day. We agreed to meet at the hidden pond surrounded by trees in the morning and see if we could help her shift.

Fear bothers me with a thousand 'what ifs' swirling through my mind. What if we can't shift back? Finn notices my worry and reassures me. *"That won't be a problem. The hardest part of shifting is coming out, not returning."*

We talk about my abduction and Ashton's plan to return me to my realm for complete healing while he tackles the Pope's downfall. We both agree that Ashton will need our help and we begin to plan how best we can provide it. I assure him that I will return early the next morning to help my dragon in shifting. I am feeling stronger and want to go for some weapon practice. I make my way to the sparring arena and observe Ashton, who is also training. I settle into the grass to watch his movements with wonder. Ashton wields his weapon with effortless precision despite the sword's weight. Unlike most warriors of his stature, who tend to be slower and rely on brute strength, he moves with remarkable agility and speed. His elven heritage gifts provide him with extraordinary advantages. Ashton is fighting two opponents when I see one of them sneaking around to attack him from behind. I summon Ashbringer to my hand without hesitation and leap into the fight, landing right behind Ashton. The rush of adrenaline is exhilarating, making my heart race, and I feel so alive that a smile spreads across my face.

I signal to the remaining warrior with a challenging gesture, my laughter echoing as I see his frustration grow. I quickly close the distance using my agility and mentally command Ashbringer to *"go hot."* I strike his sword with such force and heat that it shatters into pieces. The warrior's eyes widen in shock as he stumbles backward, but I press forward relentlessly.

Suddenly, everything became clear to me. This isn't just practice anymore; the danger before me and the need to protect Ashton turn the fight into something primal. My focus sharpens and is driven by a visceral urge. I feel an overwhelming need for this warrior to fall at my feet and die, my resolve hardening into an almost uncontrollable desire for victory.

As I continue to fight, I hear Ashton's voice commanding me to stand down, but I am too caught up in the battle to listen to him. Suddenly, he appears in front of me, pulling me in a tight embrace. He wraps his arms around me and draws me closer to his body. His voice is gentle and soothing, breaking through the fog of my rage as he looks deeply into my eyes.

My breath comes in ragged gasps, and my body begins to tremble uncontrollably. The anger I have been channeling feels almost like a living force that is rolling off me in fierce waves. Ashton's presence grounds me, but I am still struggling to regain control. He is concerned and so close to me that I can feel the warmth of his breath.

"Anwen, look at me. Just look at me." He holds me and says softly.

I look at him, and my eyes reflect the uproar of my emotions. I see that he is worried, and I realize what has happened. I dematerialize Ashbringer with a nod, and the sword vanishes from my hand. I stare at Ashton, feeling shame and relief as I struggle to understand my reactions. I am shocked that I lost control.

Ashton addresses the remaining warriors and dismisses them with a firm but respectful tone. The atmosphere is filled with tension; many of his warriors, family, and friends have suffered under the Pope's Inquisition and are determined to see him removed once and for all.

His warriors understand the lasting effects of torture at the Pope's hands. They are united in their cause, ready to stand alongside anyone who fights against their mutual enemy, *the Pope.*

Ashton guides me to a nearby bench close to the sparring area. His presence feels like a comforting anchor amidst my confusion. Everything has happened so quickly that I'm struggling to fully grasp it, but Ashton comprehends the situation perfectly. He gently explains that many warriors who have endured captivity can enter a heightened state of alert when they perceive a threat. This instinct can push them into a dangerous fight mode.

I look at him; my eyes are clouded with a mix of bewilderment and self-doubt. I nod, wondering if there is something fundamentally wrong with me. Every warrior knows that controlling one's emotions in battle is crucial, or they will lose, yet I feel like I have failed in this basic skill.

Ashton places a reassuring hand on my shoulder, "What you have experienced is a normal response given what you've been through. I'll help you work through these emotions while fighting. For now, I want you to spar only with me, alright?"

I nod as my anxiety is momentarily eased by his support. I hug him tightly and say, "When I saw him circling behind you, I felt an uncontrollable urge to protect you. I couldn't stop myself once I was in the fight."

Ashton smiles warmly, "Mated couples protect each other with fierce devotion. There's no hesitation, no holding back with us; we fight to the death to keep our mate safe. Your reaction is completely normal, Anwen. Elves are even more formidable with their cool and calculated minds in battle. We don't falter."

I nod and feel relief that he understands why I lost control of my emotions. I pull Ashton's head down for a deep and lingering kiss. As I pull away, I gently lick my lips and look up at him with a small smile, "I love you, my mate."

Ashton's eyes widen in astonishment and he takes a sharp breath, as if the weight of my words has just hit him. He closes his eyes and whispers, "You don't know how long I've wanted to hear those words from you, little one."

I look at Ashton hopefully, "Perhaps we can complete the mating ritual now?"

Ashton sighs deeply, his expression heavy with reluctance, "You don't know how difficult it is for me to say this, but we can't."

I pull him back, "Why the delay?"

He reaches out to me and pulls me close to him once more, "If I were to fall in battle against the Pope while we are fully mated, you would suffer immensely. In many mated pairs, when one dies, the other often follows soon after. I can't bear the thought of putting you in that position, little one."

I know that mated couples are bound for life, though I have never given much thought to the specifics. The idea that I might never expect to find my mate is now painfully clear, "I understand that, but I can't ignore this overwhelming need to be with you."

Ashton holds me tightly and says in a deep voice, "You're killing me; I'm desperate for you. I'll continue to do my best to ease the longing between us until the time is right, but I won't put you at risk by completing the mating ritual."

I pout and pull him away with frustration, "Fine! But I won't stop wanting or teasing you, Ashton."

Ashton smiles gently, placing her hand over his heart, "I will always love you, Anwen. You are my life's breath." He holds my hand tenderly and kisses my palm softly before we walk together toward the castle for breakfast.

As we are enjoying our meal, Banoff arrives and joins us, and his weary appearance starkly contrasts with the lively atmosphere. He looks thinner than usual, dark circles under his eyes betraying his exhaustion as he begins to outline his recent discoveries. After we finish eating, we go to the study to discuss our next moves. He reveals that he has managed to establish contact with a leader of the Knights Templar. After extensive negotiations, a secret contract is drafted between the Templars and the House of Lionsway. According to the contract, the Templars will provide ten undercover knights to aid in the fight against the Pope. These knights will infiltrate Rome and are awaiting further orders. Upon the Pope's defeat, the Templars expect to receive the religious artifacts and wealth uncovered.

Banoff also shares crucial intelligence on the Pope's current situation. The Pope commands approximately seventy troops, including fifteen Jesuits. He has also requested reinforcements from neighboring fiefdoms, which are expected to arrive within a month. Given this, the Templars recommend launching an attack within the next two weeks. Additionally, the Templars require a future favor from Ashton, the details of which will need to be fulfilled at a later date. Despite the complexities, Banoff insists that this is the best arrangement they could secure.

Ashton considers the terms thoughtfully before nodding in agreement. "I'll review the contract immediately."

Ashton is puzzled by the Pope's request for reinforcements as he turns to Banoff with a probing question, "Why is the Pope asking for more troops?"

Banoff takes a deep breath before responding, "The Templars' sources have uncovered that the Pope has formed a secret, unholy alliance with King Philip VI of France. The Pope and the King are uneasy about the growing power of the Templars, both in terms of their military strength and their land holdings. In reality, what they desire is the wealth that the Templars control. The King of France has even started spreading false rumors, painting the Templars as power-hungry and ungodly."

He continues in his grim tone, "The Pope and the King are trying to hedge their bets by amassing as many additional soldiers as they can. They hope to counter the Templars' influence and secure their positions of power by overwhelming them with sheer numbers."

Ashton is confused and says, "The Pope has previously sanctioned and supported the Templars. It doesn't make sense that he would now turn against them except that he has already shown his true colors— greed and a hunger for power."

Banoff's expression hardens as he replies, "The Pope is currently denying the rumors about the Templars, but nobody believes the deceitful, greedy bastard. His actions speak louder than his denials, and his motives are all too clear."

I interrupt frustratedly and angrily to say, "The Pope kept pressuring me to shift and control my dragon. He wanted to harness the dragon's power and magic to manipulate kings, queens, and entire nations. With such power in his hands, he would be unstoppable. His ultimate goal is to topple the monarchies and place the church in absolute control over the nations."

Ashton nods gravely, "Indeed, that is his intention. After the death of Queen Mary of England, the Pope rejected the succession of Queen Elizabeth I. Queen Elizabeth specifically asked me to keep a close watch on the Pope's ambitions. Every move he makes confirms that this is his plan."

Ashton's voice is steady and resolute as he outlines our current resources and strategy, "We have fifty of my warriors ready for battle with ten remaining behind to safeguard the castle and its grounds. The Queen has agreed to provide discreet support through a network of spies and warriors stationed in Rome, though she must remain unconnected to our cause. If King Philip and the Pope discover her involvement, they will accuse her of plotting against their countries, which could ignite a full-scale war."

He pauses for a moment and says, "The Knights Templars are formidable military strategists and will bring substantial forces to the conflict. However, we cannot involve additional Houses in our plans. The risk of our strategy being leaked to the Pope and the King of France is too great."

Banoff's face shows clear concern as he speaks, "I'm worried that the Jesuits have been scouting the area looking for ways to capture Anwen and Finn again."

Ashton reassures him in his calm voice, "I've made arrangements for us to leave for Anwen's realm tomorrow. You'll be in charge of safeguarding the castle and preparing the men for our move to Rome."

He adds with a nod, "Make sure to get some rest tonight."

Banoff grins, "I need to find my beautiful chambermaid and remind her just how much I've missed her. Then I'll be able to rest."

Ashton chuckles, and my smile widens as we fondly recall the warm and intimate moments we have witnessed between us before.

SIXTEEN

Dragon Shapeshifting

I confide in Ashton about my change of plans. Finn and I had initially intended to help my water dragon with its transformation tomorrow, but now I must tackle it immediately. Ashton's eyes show his concern as he expresses his desire to be by my side during this critical moment. My heart is pounding with uncertainty. I don't know how this change will go or what consequences might follow if it succeeds. The thought that my dragon might become threatening and endanger those around me weighs heavily on my mind. I share my anxieties with Ashton with a doubtful tone to my voice.

Ashton places a comforting hand on my shoulder, "I'll be right here with you." He promises, "We'll face whatever comes together." His presence gives me a bit of hope, that this first attempt at dragon shifting will be safe and successful.

As Ashton and I walk to the stables, I inform Finn that our plan to help the water dragon's transformation has changed. Finn is ready for the task as he joins us. We head toward the pond together to hide deep within the dense and ancient trees at the far end of the property. Maynard arrives there, too, and offers to patrol the perimeter. Her wings create a soft rustling sound as she takes flight. She promises to alert us if anyone approaches and provides a measure of comfort.

Finn begins to explain the process of calling forth the dragon's shift. *"You need to summon her."* He advises, *"Reassure her that it's safe and that another dragon shifter whom she can trust is here to assist."*

I nod, and my heart races as I undress, leaving my shift on. I step into the cool water of the pond and let the gentle ripples soothe my nerves. As soon as I am waist-deep, I close my eyes and focus inward.

"It's time to shift, my friend." I whisper to my dragon with a calm voice, *"It's safe now, and Finn is here to help us."*

I wade deeper and begin to swim slowly. The water envelops me as I move, and my mind is concentrated. Lyra's voice echoed, *"I am afraid, Anwen, but I will try."*

Suddenly, I feel a warm sensation spreading from my abdomen and stretching outward like a gentle wave. An intense light surrounds me by blocking my vision and senses. During the blinding brightness, I find myself in a serene and quiet space, able to see and hear but unable to communicate with Lyra or anyone else. As the transformation completes, Lyra emerges from me, and Finn's eyes widen in awe. Although smaller than most dragons, I radiate stunning beauty. My scales shimmer like moonlit water, captivating and graceful.

Finn tries to mind speak with me, *"Can you hear me, young dragon?"*

The dragon's head swivels toward him, and I nod *yes*. I begin to glide lazily around the pond. My movements are fluid and serene. I seem to revel in the sensation of the water cascading over me.

"I am Lyra." She introduces herself, *"I am a water dragon. My gift lies in healing and removing pain, but I must admit I'm not as skilled in combat as you might be."*

Finn smiles reassuringly at Lyra, *"That's perfectly alright, Lyra. Our goal is to help you feel comfortable and to get to know you better. Can you communicate with Anwen yet?"*

Lyra looks thoughtful and nods gently, *"I'm trying, but it seems we're having trouble connecting,"* she says.

Finn nods sympathetically, *"It's normal for this to take some time and practice for both of you. Don't worry; it will get easier."*

He then asks, *"Could you tell us a bit about yourself?"*

Lyra's eyes soften as she responds, *"I don't know much yet, but I can tell you that I adore my human and am incredibly proud of her. My strength comes from water and I can travel great distances both on the water and beneath it."* She pauses, then adds, *"I can also share my underwater breathing skills with Anwen."*

Finn's eyes widen with curiosity and admiration, *"That's extraordinary, Lyra. I've never heard of dragons and humans sharing such an ability. It's truly rare and special, just like you."*

Lyra gratefully says, *"Thank you, Finn."*

Finn then suggests, *"Would you like to try using your wings to leave the water?"*

Lyra hesitates, *"I'm not sure. I feel weak from the shift and am afraid to attempt it now."*

Finn understands her hesitation and reassures her, *"That's completely fine. You can shift back whenever you're ready."*

Ashton watches in amazement as the transformation happens. Lyra is stunning; her scales are a mesmerizing blend of pure white with bronze tips that catch the light beautifully. The water seems to embrace her, reacting as if in awe of her presence. Compact yet powerful, she glides through the pond with grace and strength. Finn and Lyra appear to be communicating telepathically, their silent exchange evident in her responsive movements.

Ashton turns to Finn with a concerned face, "Is Anwen alright?"

Finn nods reassuringly. Ashton visibly relaxes and enjoys the sight of the graceful dragon swimming. Lyra approaches Ashton. She gently stops at the edge of the pond, her eyes meeting his with a calm look.

He steps forward to delicately touch her snout, "Did you visit my dreams, Lyra?" he asks softly.

She nods.

Ashton says with gratitude, "Thank you for helping my mate."

Lyra responds with a gentle nod before slowly swimming back to the center of the pond. She communicates with Finn to indicate that she is ready to shift back. Finn explains the process to her and guides her through the steps to call forth my return. Suddenly, I hear Lyra's voice echo in my mind, urging me to *"shift."* A powerful pull jolts me, and in an instant, I find myself submerged underwater. Panic sets in as I kick desperately to reach the surface.

Lyra tells her, *"It's okay, Anwen, just breathe."*

I had forgotten about our shared ability to inhale water. As water fills my lungs, my lungs don't seize like before, and I relax, floating and enjoying the moment of calm. *"This is amazing, Lyra. Thank you for this gift."*

Ashton looks worried as he approaches the water's edge. He jumps into the pond without thinking, and his worries are clear in every splash. As I float underwater, I suddenly feel strong arms wrapping around me, pulling me toward the light above.

As I break the surface, I expel the water in my lungs and gasp for air. I am relieved that Lyra was able to dragon shift out and back in without difficulty. I just needed to remember that she enabled me to breathe underwater without panicking.

Ashton's dark hair is hovering above me as I reach out and touch his face, saying, "With all the changes happening to me, I am going to give you grey hair. Lyra blessed me with her water breathing." I watch him smile and love the crinkles that show around his eyes.

Ashton's fingers gently brush against my wet hair and say, "You and your dragon are truly amazing."

Finn and Maynard informed me that they were heading back to the castle. Ashton pulled me close. Using his strong legs and arms, he carried me to the pond's edge.

He gently supports my head, tilts it slightly, and kisses me softly as we get there. His kiss deepens to tongue thrusts into my mouth over and over with passion. I hold onto his shoulders and wrap my legs around his waist as we share an intense moment.

He stops kissing and presses his forehead against mine. "I want you, Anwen." he confesses, "My feelings for you are overwhelming, and I'm struggling to control them."

I gently untangle my legs from around him, sliding down his body. My fingers reach for him, tenderly stroking through his pants.

He hisses like he's uncomfortable, and I pause. He places his hand over mine, shows me how to stoke him, and I resume teasing him. He starts kissing me once more. I am touching him while his hand moves to my nipple, and he gently rubs and tweaks it. This sensation sends shivers through me. He moans and shows me how to increase my speed and adjust my grip on his shaft. I am enjoying the effect I have on him as he throws his head back and moans with pleasure as he rides through his orgasm.

As he recovers, he lifts me, and I wrap my legs around his waist again. He brings me up to his mouth, sucking my nipples through my shift, causing me to gasp as he nips, flicks, and draws me in.

He moves to my other breast, teasing that nipple until it peaks. He gently slides me down his body to his waist, pushing my shift aside. His fingers begin to stroke and stimulate me. I am close to my climax as he enters me with the tip of his shaft. He moves his shaft tip in and out shallowly, driving me insane with need. He continues to play me like a fine instrument with his mouth, fingers, and shaft. I reach the peak of my orgasm, crying out his name. He maintains his pace and depth, quickly approaching his release once more. He sucks hard on my nipple, groaning around it as his orgasm peaks. He withdraws his shaft and lifts me again to gently lick and suckle my nipples as we both gradually recover from our orgasms. He holds me tight against his chest and shares that it took all his willpower not to bury himself in my softness, but feeling inside me that little bit was worth the struggle.

He whispers, "Our bond is growing stronger with our love and shared moments. You mean everything to me, Anwen."

I smile at him, resting my head on his shoulder, and reply, "I've never felt so loved, safe, and open with anyone. You've set the standard so high no one else compares."

His eyes narrow slightly, a playful scowl on his lips as he squeezes my buttocks and growls, "Mine."

I laugh, teasingly licking and nipping at his neck, and respond, "Always."

SEVENTEEN

Portal Magic

The next day, we ride into Ashton's forest, the ancient trees towering above us, their branches thick with the hum of magic. I'm on Finn, his steady gait matching my own growing anticipation. Maynard perches on my shoulder, her tiny claws gripping lightly, always alert. Ashton leads the way on his warhorse, both of us in the mail, swords within easy reach. Banoff scouted ahead earlier, but the threat of Jesuits lingers like a shadow, keeping us on edge. The trail we're following is lined with small, flowering grasses, their soft colors a stark contrast to the cold steel we carry. The trees whisper in the breeze, their secrets carried on the wind, and the air smells like earth and blossoms.

Ashton guides us deeper into the forest, and we round a bend where the trail narrows, the trees closing in as if urging us to turn back. He halts and dismounts gracefully. From the leather packs fastened to his saddle, he pulls out several runes, each a different shape and color: red, blue, green, and purple. I watch him as he moves toward a small boulder, half hidden beneath a curtain of ferns. The grooves in the stone seem perfectly made for the runes as if they've been waiting for this moment for centuries.

"Stay mounted," Ashton instructs, his voice steady as he places each rune in its designated spot. "The portal will pull us through shortly."

I nod, holding Finn's reins a bit tighter as he mounts up and begins an incantation. The words are low and rhythmic, and I can feel the magic building in the air, thick and heavy. A circular, smoky portal forms in front of us, and I guide Finn closer to Ashton's horse, bracing myself for the pull. It starts as a gentle tug, then a stronger pull that wraps around us like an unseen force. In a blink, we're no longer in Ashton's forest but standing in mine – a place I know as well as I know myself.

This time, the journey through the portal feels different. There's no harsh jolt, no dizzying spin, just a smooth transition from one world to another. I take a deep breath, the familiar scents of my forest filling my lungs. There's a fleeting dizziness, but it passes quickly, leaving me feeling oddly at peace. Ashton is already dismounting, gathering the runes from a boulder similar to the one on the other side and tucking them back into his leather bag.

"That was much easier," I say, relieved. The last portal journey had been rougher, leaving us reeling.

Ashton nods, thoughtful. "The runes provide a steady power source for the portal, making the travel smoother."

"Can anyone use them?" I ask, curious.

He hesitates, then shakes his head. "I'm not sure. I've always assumed others couldn't. They were passed down to me after my parents... after they were gone. I've kept them safe ever since."

We fall into a comfortable silence as I take the lead, guiding us deeper into my forest. Ashton is quiet, likely taking in the differences between our worlds. The trees here are colossal, their branches intertwining to form a natural cathedral, sunlight filtering through in soft, golden rays. The air buzzes faintly with magic, a sensation I've always found comforting. As we move, the plants lean toward us, acknowledging our presence, and birds flit ahead, their songs a cheerful melody that I've missed. The colors around us are richer and more vibrant, as shown by the scattered mushrooms with purple caps instead of the usual red ones from Ashton's forest.

I turn in my saddle, catching Ashton's eye, and smile wide. It feels so good to be home, to be in the place where I belong. He returns my smile, and for a moment, the world feels perfect.

He rides up beside me. "How far is your castle?" he asks.

"Not far," I reply, my heart light as I start sharing the history of my home. "We're in the realm of Eldoria now. My father's lands are part of the House of Elwen. He's Lord Roderick—a widower since I was young. He raised me to take over the House when the time comes."

As I speak, I can tell Ashton understands the weight of responsibility I carry. It's a burden we both know well. I talk about my days filled with learning estate management, defense, and diplomacy with the Council of Elders and other noble Houses. Ashton listens closely, and his respect for me is evident. We've always been drawn to each other, and I'm starting to see why. We're alike in ways that matter.

He watches me as I ride, his gaze lingering. I can feel it, the way he studies me, watching me with my back straight and strong, my shoulders set with purpose. I know he's noticing the way my legs grip Finn's sides, and I can't help but think of the nights we've spent together, wrapped in each other's arms. My hair flows down my back, caught occasionally by the breeze, and I smile, knowing he's doing his best to stay focused on the path ahead.

We round a bend, and the forest gives way to a hard-packed road that leads uphill. At the top of a small mountain stands my castle, its silver-white walls gleaming in the sunlight. Blue flags fly from the turrets, and the drawbridge is lowered, spanning the river that circles the castle before cascading into a waterfall downstream. Trees in full bloom surround the stronghold, their pink and white flowers a soft contrast against the stone. As we ride closer, I spot the homes scattered across the valley below, the neat rows of crops, and the sound of children's laughter carried on the wind.

Suddenly, a long, straight arrow thuds into the ground in front of Ashton's horse. The animal rears and Ashton draws his sword, shouting for me to run. But I don't. Instead, I turn in my saddle, smiling calmly.

"It's alright," I assure him, though he's still tense. Another arrow strikes the ground near his horse, and he halts, his grip on his sword tight.

I raise my arm, signaling to stop the arrows. "It's just a precaution," I explain. "They were testing to see if I was a prisoner. It's how they ensure I'm not under duress."

He sheaths his sword, his heart still pounding—I can see it in his eyes—as we continue toward the drawbridge. As we cross into the courtyard, the familiar scent of home fills my senses, and I feel a surge of relief.

EIGHTEEN

Runes, Stones, and Magic

As we enter the castle's inner courtyard, the familiar sight of my father, Roderick, waiting on the entrance step sends a ripple of tension through me. His presence is commanding, and his expression is unreadable, as always. I gently nudge Finn toward the stable, and I hear Ashton's horse following behind. We dismount, and the relief in Finn and Maynard is palpable; they've been on edge for too long, and it's good to see them relax. As I tend to Finn, brushing his coat and murmuring soft words of comfort, I feel Ashton's eyes on me.

"My father is stern but fair," I say, placing a hand on Ashton's arm. "Don't be surprised by how he acts. He wants what's best for me and our House."

Ashton nods, but I can tell he's curious about the relationship between my father and me. I'm not sure I can explain fully how it feels to be the daughter of Roderick Elwen, with all the expectations and responsibilities that come with it. But we'll have time for that later. For now, we need to face him together.

We walk toward my father, our footsteps echoing in the stone courtyard. As we get closer, Roderick turns and strides inside without a word, and we follow him into his study. The room is exactly as I remember: lined with ancient tomes, the scent of old parchment and polished wood filling the air. I introduce Ashton formally, then launch into an update on everything that's happened, carefully omitting any mention of our relationship and my captivity at the hands of the Pope. I know my father well enough to tread cautiously.

Throughout my recounting, Roderick listens in silence, his face a mask of impassivity. When I finish, he motions for us to sit, his gaze turning to Ashton with the piercing intensity he reserves for those he's assessing.

"What realm do you come from?" my father begins, his tone sharp as he questions Ashton about his holdings, affiliations, and duties. I watch Ashton handle the inquiries with calm precision, though I can sense his underlying tension.

Then, Roderick turns to me, his voice laced with disappointment. "Why did you bring Ashton back to our realm, Anwen? I'm surprised you didn't take control of your situation and return home faster. You have many duties waiting for you, and Salsabar has been inquiring about you since your disappearance."

I straighten, feeling the familiar weight of his expectations. "I'm aware of my duties and will resume them immediately. And you know how I feel about Salsabar."

"He's from a fine House. The Council of Elders passed judgment that you will marry as soon as possible due to your duel challenge," Roderick replies, his eyes narrowing slightly. "Combining our estates will make us even more powerful, Anwen."

Ashton sits quietly, observing the dynamic between my father and me. I can feel his disapproval of how formal and distant our interaction is as if I'm not his daughter but merely a vessel for his ambitions. A part of me burns with shame that Ashton has to witness this, and I'm angry that my father is already pushing Salsabar on me again.

I rise abruptly, needing to escape the stifling atmosphere. "Excuse me, but I need to check on a few things. Ashton, I'll make sure someone shows you to your quarters and informs you when we'll break our fast." Without waiting for a response, I leave the room, my heart heavy with unspoken words and unresolved tensions.

As I walk away, I can feel Ashton's eyes on me, but I know he'll stay behind to face whatever challenge my father throws at him next. As soon as I'm gone, Roderick shifts his focus entirely to Ashton, his eyes cold and calculating.

"You do realize," my father says, his voice low, "that being human prevents you from having any permanent relationship with my daughter. She has responsibilities to our House and Kingdom, and she doesn't have the luxury of choosing her life mate. She can have physical relations with whomever she wants, but she will mate with an elf male according to our political and House standing, not for something as trite as love."

Ashton's face remains impassive, but I know him well enough to sense the anger simmering beneath the surface. "I'm well aware of how the human world works with arranged marriages and politics; Eldoria and your House appear to be the same. I wanted to ensure Anwen returned home safely and discuss a possible alliance between our Houses. It could be profitable for us both."

My father arches an eyebrow. "How did you make the portal appear? I would assume magic was needed, and humans do not have magic."

Ashton doesn't miss a beat. "It's a simple method of using runes and an incantation that my parents passed down to me. No magic is required. I have no idea how my parents learned this, but it's useful for time travel."

My father leans back in his chair, intrigued. "That time travel could be beneficial. Can you share the runes with others?"

"No, only I can use the runes," Ashton replies smoothly.

"Interesting," Roderick muses, his eyes narrowing slightly. "What is your proposal for our Houses' alliance?"

Ashton smiles, a calculating gleam in his eye. "Just a simple sharing of resources. I need to rid my realm of a particularly power-hungry Pope. My Queen can't be involved, or it'll lead to an all-out war between our countries. I've already amassed additional warriors, spies, and logistical support, but I need more soldiers. If you can supply troops to bolster my resistance, I'll be able to defeat the Pope and stop his quest for total power and control of our realm."

Roderick's eyebrows rise slightly as he considers the proposal. "That is quite an undertaking. I'm unsure how this affects my realm or how it would benefit my House to help."

"Other realms would want this ability," Ashton continues, his voice steady. "They might want to time travel to your realm. Your world would no longer be sequestered away from others; they may want to take your realm. I'm willing to share my time travel abilities with your world and only your world. I'm sure your leaders would be interested."

I can imagine my father's mind working, calculating the potential gains and risks. This could elevate our House's standing and open up possibilities that have never been available before.

Then, Ashton drops the final card on the table. "I have one request: Anwen. I want her as my mate. If you accept my proposal, our Houses will be bound together, and you'll have an even stronger political position with the House of Elders. A secure position no one can take from you or me."

There's a pause, and I can almost hear my father weighing his options. "I'm interested in your offer but need time to consider it. You're welcome to stay until we work through the proposal you've presented. I'll need to speak with Anwen as well."

Ashton stands, his posture confident. "I must leave within a day. The offer will not be available after I leave." He turns and walks out the door, determination in every step as he seeks me out.

I'm in the middle of discussing food and grain stocks and castle mason work with various heads of the House when he finds me. I can feel his presence before I see him, a warmth that wraps around me like a cloak. I continue asking questions and making notes, but I'm aware of him leaning against the doorframe, watching me. Finally, I lift my head, catching his scent in the air, and turn to see him smiling at me. My heart skips a beat, and I quickly excuse everyone in the room.

Once we're alone, he closes the door and strides over to me, sitting beside me on the bench. His eyes search mine, and I reach up to touch his cheek, the connection between us sparking like it always does. I lean in and press my lips to his, a soft, lingering kiss that deepens as he takes control. We pull away, both of us breathing heavily, the air between us charged with unspoken desire.

"How I wish for true privacy," Ashton murmurs, his voice rough with longing. "I want you in every way possible, for hours, just us."

I turn my back to his front, leaning into him, savoring the feeling of his strong arms around me. His hands find my breasts, teasing my nipples with slow strokes, pinches, and tugs that send shivers down my spine. I start to squirm against him, feeling his arousal press into me, the tension building between us.

After a moment, he stops and turns me to face him, his eyes dark with desire. "We need to stop, or it'll be obvious what we're up to here."

I nod, reluctantly pulling away. He then shares the details of his conversation with my father, and my eyes widen as he explains his plan.

I can hardly believe what I'm hearing. "You asked to mate with me as part of your proposal?"

Ashton nods, watching my reaction closely. "I know your father would never agree to you mating a human, but I dangled my time travel ability. They might make an exception. This is a gamble, but removing the Pope from power is necessary."

"I need to be with you to help protect your back through this," I say, my voice firm. "Please don't deny me the ability to be with you. I'm almost fully healed now. It will take days for my father to gain permission for this alliance."

Ashton turns to me, his voice steady with purpose. "I need to test something with you first. We need to ride to the portal area, and I want to see if you can use the runes and incantation to open it. We're close to being mated—it might just work. If it does, you can bring additional warriors with you. We'll meet up at a designated point. When can we try?"

I consider his words for a few moments before answering. "Tonight, when it's dark. We can reach the portal without being seen. I'll meet you at the stable."

Ashton nods, stepping closer to me, our shared breath mingling in the space between us. He pulls me into an embrace, his hands tracing the curve of my waist, then sliding lower to squeeze my buttocks. His body presses against mine with a heated urgency, his lips finding the sensitive shell of my ear. He nips at it, his tongue flicking out to soothe the playful bite, eliciting a soft moan from me. As his mouth trails down to my neck, his teeth grazing the tender skin, I arch into him with need, both of us breathing heavily, desire to ignite between us.

Our moment was abruptly shattered by a knock at the door. We froze, the sound of another knock making us step apart with a silent laugh. "Is anyone in there?" comes a voice from outside. I take a moment to compose myself, adjusting my clothing and taking a deep breath. "Yes, I'll be out shortly," I call back.

After a few moments to cool down, I open the door to find Salsabar standing there, his expression twisted with irritation. He sniffs the air, his eyes narrowing as they settle on me. "What do we have here, Anwen? A new human pet?"

I laugh, dismissing the notion with a wave of my hand. "Ah, no. Let it go, Sal. You don't want to mess with Ashton."

Salsabar's gaze flicks back to me, a sneer curling his lip. "I don't mind you having a pet. We all have needs, don't we? But a human? Really? I'm surprised he can even fulfill your needs."

I exchange a look with Ashton, and we both burst into laughter. My eyes sparkled with amusement as I turned back to Salsabar. "No need to worry yourself, Sal. We don't have any problems in that department."

Dismissing the interaction, we start walking past him when Salsabar blocks our path, his eyes locked on Ashton. "Go home, human. This is our realm, and Anwen is mine."

Ashton had let me handle the situation so far, but there were limits to his patience. He quickly assesses Salsabar, noting the elf's height and muscular build. But there is something about the way Salsabar holds himself that betrays his lack of real experience in battle: It is no warrior's poise. Ashton meets Salsabar's gaze with a calm, unyielding stare. "Some men are born leaders and warriors; some men have the gift of communication and become diplomats. What are your strengths? All I see is a boy pretending to be a man."

Salsabar recoils slightly, a sneer forming on his lips. "I won't fight you inside Anwen's home, but you will regret crossing me today."

Ashton isn't done. "Anytime, any place. Anwen is mine, and I do not share." He moves forward, hand resting on the hilt of his sword, his presence alone enough to make Salsabar step aside. As Ashton reaches for my hand, a sense of victory washes over him. Triumphantly, we walk down the corridor together, his thumb gently stroking the back of my hand. Smiling beside him, I felt my love for Ashton deepen, realizing once again how much he truly meant to me.

NINETEEN

Dragon Genetics

Night has fully fallen, wrapping the world in a heavy, suffocating darkness as Ashton and I draw closer to the portal's location. The shadows seem to press in around us, thick with tension and the promise of danger. Finn won't stop talking—his questions tumble out in rapid succession, all about Lyra. How is she? Can she speak to him yet? I answer him, but my mind is only half on his words. Maynard has flown ahead scouting. My eyes are constantly scanning the trees, the rocks, and every dark corner where something—or someone—might be lurking. Ashton is beside me, equally alert, his gaze sharp as he watches our surroundings with that quiet intensity I've come to rely on.

Then, without warning, four shadowy figures spring from the darkness. It happens so fast—a blur of black-clad bodies rushing us. Finn reacts first, his powerful jaws snapping around one attacker with a ferocity that surprises even me. Ashton is already engaged with two of them, his sword flashing in the dim light. The fourth figure grabs me from behind just as I'm turning to help Ashton. The cold press of steel grazes my neck as my assailant hisses in my ear, "Don't call your sword, or I'll snap your neck."

For a split second, I freeze, weighing my options. Then, without hesitation, I drop all my weight, letting my legs give out beneath me. The sudden move catches him off guard, and I feel his grip falter. I slam my elbow back, aiming for his crotch with all the strength I can muster. He grunts, a low, pained hiss escaping him, and his hold on me loosens just enough. I twist free and leap to my feet, ready to summon Ashbringer—but then I see Ashton.

He's bleeding, his sword arm slick with red, the two attackers circling him like wolves. Finn isn't faring much better; he's still holding onto his attacker, but blood is matting the fur on his chest. Rage explodes inside me, white-hot and all-consuming. My vision narrows, and all I can think of is protecting them, saving them.

"Shift," I scream inside my head, and I feel Lyra stirring, ready to burst forth. She's been watching, waiting for me to let her out, and now she surges to the surface. A swirl of white smoke envelops me, and then Lyra is there, powerful and furious. She calls down rain in an instant, the sky splitting open as she opens her mouth, releasing a bolt of lightning that streaks toward Finn's attacker. At the same time, her tail whips around, the barbed end slicing through the air to land with a sickening crunch on my assailant, splitting him clean in two. The smell of scorched earth and ash fills the air as the lightning-struck attacker crumbles into nothing.

Finn begins his shift, his form expanding, growing until he towers over the battlefield as a massive dragon. Lyra doesn't hesitate; she charges the two remaining attackers who are still trying to take down Ashton. She grabs one by the head, her jaws clamping down with a sickening crunch. Blood sprays, warm and metallic, as she decapitates him in one swift motion. She turns toward the other, but Ashton is already there, driving his sword through the attacker's chest with a fierce determination.

Lyra's eyes find Ashton's, searching for signs of injury, and when she sees the gash on his arm, she moves to him without a second thought. Her tears fall onto the wound, and I watch as his flesh knits itself back together, the pain leaving his eyes as he smiles up at her. "Thank you, Lyra," he says, his voice soft with gratitude. "For everything."

She bows her head, a gesture of acknowledgment, before turning to Finn. He's fully shifted now, standing taller and heavier than Lyra, his golden eyes watching her with a quiet intensity. I feel the connection between them, a faint tickle in my mind as Finn reaches out. *"Are you okay?"* he asks, his voice gentle.

"I'm calmer now," Lyra replies, her own voice softer, the anger draining away. Finn looks at her, his gaze appreciative. *"You fought well, Lyra. I'm proud of you."*

She dips her head, a flush of warmth filling me at his praise. *"Let me heal your wounds,"* she offers, seeing the gashes on his chest.

Finn shakes his head, his voice firm but kind. *"No, these are minor wounds. They'll heal quickly."* Before she can argue, I feel her beginning to retreat, the edges of my consciousness sharpening as Lyra shifts back, leaving me standing there, disoriented and breathing hard.

The first thing I do is look for Ashton. He's there, gathering the reins of his horse, his movements calm and controlled despite everything. Relief floods through me, so overwhelming that I nearly stagger. I rush to him, grabbing his shoulders, needing to feel him solid and real beneath my hands. "Are you okay?" I ask, my voice trembling with the effort of holding back tears.

He smiles down at me, that same steady smile that always calms the storm inside me. "Yes, thanks to you and Lyra." He pulls me into a kiss, hard and desperate, like he needs the reassurance as much as I do. My mind replays the image of the attackers circling him, their cruel eyes fixed on his bleeding arm, and I shudder. I almost lost him.

We gather ourselves quickly, checking the area for any remaining threats. Maynard had flown back as quickly as she could when she heard my call to shift. Finn, now back in his horse form, sniffs the air, his nostrils flaring as he searches for any lingering danger. The bodies of the attackers lie scattered around us, all elves, but with no identifying marks or clues as to who sent them. It's another mystery, another question added to the growing list of things we don't understand. Who in this realm wants us dead?

We find the portal stone hidden in a large bush, its surface cool and smooth under my fingers as Ashton hands me the runes. He talks me through the process, guiding me as I place each rune carefully into its designated spot on the stone. When I speak the incantation, the air hums with energy, and slowly, a portal begins to open before us. I can hardly believe it's real—this magical, shimmering doorway that wasn't there a moment ago. Ashton grins at me, his eyes sparkling with excitement. Even Finn, usually so stoic, can't help but mutter, *"That's powerful magic."*

Ashton shows me how to close the portal, removing one of the runes and watching as the doorway slowly seals itself shut. We gather the runes, and Ashton explains that they need to recharge in the sun before we can use them again. The rain has stopped, leaving the air cool and fresh as we mount our horses and begin the ride back to the castle.

As we ride, I speak silently to Lyra, thanking her for what she did, for protecting Ashton and healing his wounds. *"I'll always help you,*

Anwen," she replies, her voice soft and warm in my mind. *"And those you care for."*

Ashton and I spend the ride back discussing the attack, trying to piece together who could be behind it and why. Ashton mentions that he tried to taunt some information out of his attackers, but they didn't give him anything useful. I tell him about the threat my attacker made, about how he warned me not to call Ashbringer forward or he would snap my neck. Ashton stiffens at that, his eyes darkening with anger. "What did you do?" he asks, his voice low and dangerous.

I can't help but grin as I remember. "I dropped all my weight and elbowed him in the balls." The memory makes me laugh, and after a moment, Ashton joins in, his laughter deep and rumbling. Even Finn and Lyra seem to be snickering in the background of my mind. I shrug, still grinning. "Hey, it works every time!" That sets off another round of laughter, and for a moment, the tension lifts, replaced by the simple joy of being alive.

When we reach the castle, we take care of the horses, making sure they're settled before heading inside. As we leave the stables, Ashton pulls me into his arms, his expression serious. "Who knows about Ashbringer in this realm?" he asks, his voice low and urgent.

I think for a moment, trying to recall who might have that knowledge. "Just about everyone in our House and Salsabar," I reply, meeting his gaze.

His eyebrows shoot up, and he gives me a long, hard look. "No," I say quickly, realizing what he's thinking. "He wouldn't. He wants me for my future holdings. He wouldn't risk losing that by killing me."

Ashton's jaw tightens as he considers that. "Maybe they weren't after you. Maybe they wanted to kill me."

The thought sends a chill down my spine, but it makes sense. We enter the castle just as Salsabar and my father are leaving the study. My father's eyes narrow as he sees us, and Salsabar sneers, "Where have you both been? Probably rutting in the stables."

Ashton moves so fast that he's just a blur, his fist connecting with Salsabar's jaw in a single, powerful strike. I watch as Salsabar crumples to the ground, and Ashton stands over him, fists clenched, his entire body radiating tension. I reach out, placing a hand on his arm, trying to calm him. He turns to me, eyes still blazing with anger, but my touch seems to ground him. My father, who had been silently observing the whole scene, just stared at Ashton for a moment before turning away and walking off without a word.

"I won't tolerate him disrespecting you," Ashton says, his voice firm and unyielding.

I can't help but smile at his protectiveness. "I know. Over the years, no one has stood up to him but me."

"Why?" Ashton asks, his brow furrowed, clearly not understanding why I'd have to face someone like Salsabar alone for so long.

"His father is a senior member of the Council of Elders," I explain, the words tasting bitter as they leave my mouth. "Many are afraid to stand up to him, fearing retribution from his father."

Ashton's eyes darken further. "He'll learn to watch his words. I'll make it worse for him each time if he doesn't."

We leave Salsabar on the floor and make our way to the kitchen for a quick snack. The chef is shutting down for the night, but she stops when we walk in, her face lighting up as she sees me. She smiles affectionately and places a plate of cookies on the table. Turning to Ashton, she asks, "What can I get you?"

"A sandwich would be great," he replies, and she immediately starts making it.

I reach for a cookie, take a bite, and savor the sweet, comforting taste. Ashton's sandwich is ready soon after, and he thanks her with a smile. She nods, hanging up her apron before leaving us alone in the kitchen.

As we eat, I catch Ashton watching me. I can't resist teasing him a little, so I lick the edge of my cookie, then grin and nip a piece off with my teeth. The look on his face is priceless, and I burst out laughing. "Now you know how you made me feel when you did that to me," I say, still chuckling.

We finish our snack and head back to the main hall, but Salsabar is nowhere to be seen. Relieved, we climb the stairs to our rooms. When we reach my door, I hesitate for a moment before asking, "Will you come in?"

He follows me inside, and as he looks around, his eyes land on a picture of a woman with my father. "Is that your mother?" he asks.

"Yes," I reply softly, feeling a pang of sorrow. "I don't know much about her; father says it pains him to speak of her."

"How did she pass?" Ashton's voice is gentle, full of concern.

"She was traveling to our capital, and her party was attacked. All were killed. They never caught the attackers." The words are hard to say, and I feel a deep ache in my chest.

He reaches for me, pulling me into a comforting embrace. "I wish I knew her," I whisper, the loss of a mother I never met weighing heavily on me.

Lyra's voice whispers faintly in my mind, *"Your mother had to have a dragon, Anwen. It is genetic, passed from the female to her offspring. She would have mated with a dragon shifter. Your father is not your sire."*

I gasped, startled. "Are you sure, Lyra?"

"Yes," she responds, her tone firm. "There is no way I could have become your dragon otherwise."

"Oh, my gods," I breathe, sinking into the nearest chair as the revelation crashes over me. I look up at Ashton, the shock clear on my face, and explain to him what Lyra just told me.

Ashton's eyes widen as he starts piecing things together. "Does your culture accept dragon shifters?"

I shake my head, my heart pounding. "No. There are no dragons in our realm now. They were hunted to extinction because our cultures clashed. The dragons could shapeshift into males but needed to bond with our females to procreate. The Council of Elders forbade this, which led to the dragons being wiped out. They fought back in the Great War, but they were overwhelmed by elf magic and numbers."

"Then your mother would have had dragon-shifter genetics," Ashton says, his voice thoughtful. "Maybe that's why your father doesn't share memories of her with you."

Lyra's voice echoes in my mind again, *"He is correct, Anwen. Your mother may have been hunted and killed if they knew she had dragon-shifter genetics to pass on. Other dragon shifters may have survived in this realm besides Finn."*

Ashton frowns, deep in thought. "Why wasn't Finn hunted and killed with his dragon genetics?"

"Finn was viewed as an anomaly," I explain, the pieces starting to fit together in my mind. "He could only shift to horse form, not as a man, so his ability to affect the elf's genetics wasn't an issue. His breeding with horses didn't pass along his dragon genetics. The Council of Elders deemed him safe for breeding programs, but I was the only one allowed to keep him."

"So no one knows why Finn has dragon genetics?" Ashton asks, his voice full of curiosity.

"Exactly," I say with a sigh. "And neither does Finn."

I stand and walk to the window, staring out into the night. Ashton comes over, wrapping his arms around me, pulling me close, and tucking my head against his chest. His warmth and strength are a comfort, but the pain in my heart remains. "Talk to me, little one," he whispers.

"When we finish helping your realm, we need to find out what happened to my mother and who was responsible," I say, my voice trembling with emotion.

"We will," Ashton promises, his voice steady and reassuring. "They're dead men walking, those who wronged your mother and the dragon shapeshifters."

Lyra's voice joins in, *"I will help you, Anwen."*

"Thank you," I whisper, holding onto Ashton tightly as grief for a mother I never knew washes over me.

The next morning, I woke up with a heavy heart. I immediately mind-speak with Finn and Maynard, sharing last night's revelations. As I dress, Maynard lands on my windowsill, nuzzling me affectionately before flying off. I'm so grateful to have such loyal friends who always have my back.

There's a knock at the door, and I open it with a smile, expecting Ashton, but it's my father. My smile fades, and I turn away, pulling my hair up as I watch him in the mirror. I love my father despite his strictness, and I've always believed he had my best interests at heart. But now, doubt creeps in, making me question everything.

Roderick watches me as he sits in a chair, crossing his legs. "I assume Ashton shared his proposal to join alliances?" he asks, his tone unreadable.

"Yes," I reply, keeping my voice steady. "Any word from the High Council?"

"A rider arrived early this morning with a missive," he says, his eyes narrowing slightly. "They are most interested in Ashton's ability to time travel, but they want more time for questions."

"There is no time," I say firmly, turning to face him. "They need to decide by today."

He nods, acknowledging my urgency. "They understand and have permitted me to provide additional warriors. However, my warriors are forbidden to use their magic and must glamour their ears at all times. They are to return to our realm immediately once the mission is completed. Our warriors will report to you alone. In return for our support, Ashton will provide time travel for whomever the Council of Elders chooses – though they need more information from Ashton before finalizing this part of the agreement. Ashton also requested that you mate with him as part of this deal. Are you aware of that?"

"Yes," I say calmly, meeting his gaze. "And I agree to the mating."

Roderick's eyes narrow further. "The Council is concerned about the offspring being part human and part elf – our laws are clear that this is outlawed in our realm. They will agree to the mating, but the children will not be allowed to live in Eldoria; they must stay in the human realm. Do you agree to this?"

I don't answer immediately, feeling the weight of his words pressing down on me.

There's another knock at the door, and I say, "Enter." Ashton walks in, his presence filling the room. He ignores my father, his eyes only on me, and pulls me into his arms. I lean into him, sighing in relief at his touch.

Roderick watches us with a cold, calculating expression. "I was just ensuring my daughter was aware your proposal included her," he says with a hint of sarcasm.

"I already knew and accepted Ashton as my mate," I reply, my voice firm.

Ashton gives my side a reassuring squeeze and stares down at my father. "Anwen can fill you in on the Council's decisions regarding your proposal," Roderick says, turning toward the door. As he reaches for the handle, Ashton speaks up.

"It's a shame that dragons were exterminated in this realm," Ashton says, his tone casual but with an underlying challenge.

My father stops, looking back at Ashton with a hard expression. "Yes, it is," he says, his voice clipped. "The dragons should have stayed with their kind." And with that, he leaves.

Ashton's grip on me tightens slightly, and I can tell he's holding back his anger. "He's hiding something," Ashton mutters, echoing the suspicion I've felt growing in my heart.

"Yes, he is," I agree, leaning into him for comfort. "But whatever it is, we'll uncover the truth together. I can't trust a word he says anymore."

Ashton turns into my embrace, his lips brushing against mine in a tender kiss. "Good morning, little one," he murmurs, his voice soft and warm. I tug him closer, a spark of desire flickering inside me. I pull his head down, capturing his lips in a long, slow kiss, savoring the moment. When we finally part, his eyes are twinkling with amusement. "Miss me much?" he asks.

I bite my lower lip, feeling a thrill at his reaction. He groans softly. "Not fair," he says, but his smile betrays his enjoyment. I can't help but smile back as I fill him in on the Council's response to his proposal.

We make our way downstairs for breakfast, the morning sun casting a gentle glow through the windows. As we eat, Ashton tells me he's leaving today to finalize plans and preparations for the upcoming attack. I nod in agreement. "I've selected the warriors myself," I say. "Once they're briefed and packed, we'll cross to your realm and head to Rome as planned," I spoke with Finn and Maynard about the plans, and they both assured me they were ready. "I'll discuss shapeshifting strategies with Lyra and Finn," I add, "We need to keep their abilities a secret for as long as we can."

We head to the stable where Ashton's war horse stands, impatiently stamping its feet. Finn is waiting in his stall, and I take the bridle, fastening it gently but firmly. As we walk out together, Ashton slips up behind me, nipping playfully at my neck. "I'll finish our mating soon," he says with a low, throaty whisper. "I can't wait to hear you scream my name."

I laugh, and the sound is light and teasing. "It might be you screaming my name," I retort. He stops, turning me toward him, and gives me a long, tender kiss, his forehead resting against mine. "Please be careful, little one," he says, his voice earnest. "I love you."

I touch his face, my heart swelling with affection. "I will," I promise. "Stay safe for me." He nods and mounts his horse, his figure already starting to blend into the morning light. I grab a tuft of Finn's mane and swing myself up onto his back, skipping the saddle in my eagerness. We ride side by side, the cool air rushing past us, heading toward the forest portal.

When we reach the portal stone, Ashton dismounts and retrieves the leather pouch holding the runes. He begins placing them onto the stone, his movements precise and practiced. The air hums with energy as he completes the incantation and steps through the portal. I gather the runes, slip them back into the pouch, and mount Finn once more as we ride back toward the castle. A pang of longing tugs at me. I'm already missing my mate.

TWENTY

Paladin and Dragon Honor

I prepare Finn for travel with a practiced efficiency. The morning chill lingers as I make my way into the castle to pack my supplies. There's a pressing need to gather the warriors and brief them for the impending battle. I left the runes with Finn for safekeeping. As I step inside, my father and Salsabar are waiting in the main keep. A shiver of unease runs down my spine; something about this feels off.

Salsabar blocks my path, his hand raised in a gesture of command. "Anwen," he begins, his voice dripping with disdain, "I'm quite upset that you've chosen to mate with that human. I expected better taste from you. Despite your questionable judgment in selecting a mate, I'm still interested in our union."

My mouth falls open in disbelief. I can hardly believe the audacity of his words. "I've been honest with you, yet you seem to disregard everything I say. I have no interest in you—none whatsoever. Is that clear enough?" I glance at my father, whose face remains as impassive as ever, offering no clue to his thoughts. "I don't have time for this," I say, frustration edging my voice. "I need to assemble my warriors for the battle in the human realm."

Salsabar stands tall, his gaze unyielding. "I forbid you to leave this realm." Instinctively, I sidestep into a defensive stance, summoning Ashbringer to my hand. "I don't care what you want, Salsabar. Move out of my way."

I telepathically reach out to Finn and Maynard. *"Maynard, Finn, you need to escape with the runes. Find a place to hide. I'll contact you soon. Lyra, be prepared to fight and fly out if necessary."* Their alarm is palpable, but they acknowledge my orders.

I turn my attention back to my father. "Do you support this?" I ask. He sighs, his expression a mask of indifference. "Anwen, I've indulged you too much. It's time for you to accept your responsibilities. The Council of Elders decreed that you should marry immediately. To expand our lands and holdings, you must mate with an elf—preferably Salsabar. It's unfortunate you've entangled yourself with a human, but the runes for time travel have elevated our House in the Council's eyes. You will not embarrass me; you will follow my orders. Now, where are the runes?"

"Somewhere safe," I reply.

A bitter realization washes over me. I've never truly seen my father for what he is—a manipulative figure pulling strings for his own advantage. I was naive to think otherwise. Now that I know he is not my father, his disdain and behaviors make sense. They never viewed me as a threat, a grave mistake on their part.

Keeping Ashbringer at the ready, I begin to back away from the main hall; my senses alert for any sign of attack. As I reach the courtyard, I'm met by the castle's warriors arrayed against me. Archers are stationed on the back wall, their arrows trained on me. Lyra's voice rings in my mind, warning me about the archers. "Where is the honor of the Paladin?" I call out, my voice echoing through the courtyard. "Have you forgotten what it means to be a warrior?"

The Sargeant of Arms steps forward. "We cannot allow humans and dragons within our realm. You've broken our laws, and we must prevent you from continuing this path."

"You act as judge and jury without knowing the full story, old friend," I retort.

I command Ashbringer to "go hot," and Finn arrives in dragon form, roaring as he scorches the archers with his fire. I leap into the fray, battling my way through the first line of warriors toward Finn. Lyra waits, poised to shift only when it's safe. Maynard circles above, alerting me to any approaching threats. We're a formidable team, unyielding and resolute.

I hear Salsabar and my father shouting for me to stop, their voices filled with frustration. Blood splatters around me as I fight, a relentless and emotionless force. My blade finds its mark with precision, and I advance toward the Sargeant of Arms. He looks at me with regret. "I'm sorry, Anwen, but I cannot let you leave."

I narrow my eyes, silent and detached. There's no room for sentiment in this battle. As we clash, his balance falters momentarily when one of his own men, trying to evade Finn's flames, pushes him from behind. Seizing the opportunity, I leap, slicing downward with a decisive strike that decapitates him instantly. I tell Lyra, "Shift." She transforms and takes to the sky with a powerful roar. Finn and Lyra soar toward the mountains, their forms fading into the distance.

Back at his castle, Ashton attends to his warhorse and dons his heavy armor. Banoff briefs him on the progress of their plans. "A rider arrived this morning," Banoff reports. "The Queen's spy and the Knights Templar are on their way to Rome from various routes. Many will stay in the Roman Ghetto, while others are spread throughout the city. Our warriors should be nearing Rome."

Ashton reflects on his first visit to Rome, recalling the Pope's decree that was confining Jewish believers to a walled ghetto with a single entry and exit. He thanks Banoff for keeping everything on track and shares his observations about Anwen's father, Salsabar, and the political landscape of Eldoria. Banoff whistles softly. "That's a lot of politics to handle in a short time. Do you trust their word?"

"No," Ashton admits, "but I have no choice but to proceed with the offer. Anwen will join us in Rome soon with her warriors." They agree that Banoff should remain at the castle as a secure fallback during the battle. Ashton finishes his meal, packs supplies onto his horse, and rides out toward Rome.

Lyra and Finn approach a high mountain plateau. Maynard, having scouted ahead, confirms it's safe to land. Being quiet and introspective, I feel troubled. We circle the landing area before touching down. I ask Lyra to *"shift,"* and she stands in a large, flat clearing on the mountain, gazing out over the valleys and forests below. Finn remains in dragon form while Maynard lands on her shoulder, nuzzling her neck. Absently, I run my fingers over my hawk's head.

Finn's voice echoes in her mind. *"Are you okay, Anwen?"*

Taking a deep breath, I turn to Finn and reply, "This realm will regret its treachery against my mother, the dragon shifters, and me. I will not fail my mate or my friends. We need a new plan for the human realm."

I instruct Maynard to keep a lookout for any activity around the portal. As I explore the area, I find a cave nestled into the cliffside. Finn shapeshifts and joins me as I investigate. The cave entrance is just wide enough for Finn in horse form, but once inside, it opens up to a spacious, towering interior. I move toward the back, where the sound of dripping water leads me to a large pool.

Finn starts clearing rocks toward a middle section of the cave, revealing an opening in the ceiling. Meanwhile, Maynard hunts for our dinner. As I continue to explore, I notice drawings on the cave walls—scenes of dragons battling warriors with fire, ice, and magic. Armies clash against dragons with magic, mechanical dragons, bows, arrows, and swords. The historical conflict between elves and dragons is vividly depicted, and it breaks my heart to witness such senseless bloodshed. I take a moment to grieve for my lost family and comrades, allowing my sorrow to wash over me. I deeply miss my mate, feeling a profound sense of loss.

Finn takes a chance and shapeshifts into his dragon form, the tunnel barely accommodating his large frame. I watch, a hint of concern creeping into my thoughts. "What if you get stuck?" I ask. His head swivels toward me, and he attempts a dragon's smile, revealing a fearsome array of teeth. He turns back, focusing on the rocks, and unleashes a stream of fire that turns them red, then white. After heating the rocks, he reverts to his horse form and trots out of the cave to gather some lumber.

Maynard swoops in, carrying two rabbits in her talons. She drops them and quickly takes off again. I retrieve my knife from my boot and start preparing the rabbits for cooking. Finn returns with the wood, and I set up a makeshift spit to roast the rabbits. Maynard reappears, this time with two large fish, which I clean and prepare. The food roasts over the fire as we gather around it, discussing our next moves. Maynard reports that warriors are starting to gather near the portal area, heightening our urgency. We evaluate our plans, discard a few, and continue to strategize our approach to and through the portal.

Finn leaves to graze on fresh grass while I settle in for a brief nap. Maynard takes on guard duty. When Finn returns, I rouse everyone and suggest we bed down for the night.

In the middle of the night, I feel a gentle breath against my cheek, then my neck. Lyra's voice whispers, *"Don't be startled; open your eyes."* I crack open my eyelids and see a small blue dragon with bright azure eyes gazing at me. "Hi, Blue," I whisper. The little dragon pulls back and scurries to the back of the cave, trembling in a corner. I rise quickly, moving to the back of the cave, and see Blue shaking, trying to hide. Dropping to my knees, I extend a hand and speak softly. "I won't hurt you. Did you know we're dragons, too?" Blue's eyes widen, and he shakes his head in surprise. "Would you like to meet our dragons?" I ask. His response is a quick, eager nod, and he cautiously approaches me.

I stand, and both Finn and Lyra are observing the interaction. I introduce Blue to my friends and explain that he wants to meet our dragons. We step outside into the chilly, dark night where there's ample room for dragons. Finn shifts first, his massive form casting a shadow over Blue. The little dragon steps back, gazing up at Finn in awe. Finn communicates with me telepathically, revealing that Blue is a male dragon. Lyra asks to shift, and I allow it. She transforms, and Blue approaches her, rubbing his head against her leg as Lyra chuckles. Blue tells her she's beautiful and he likes her.

Through our conversation, Finn and Lyra discover that Blue's parents are dragon shapeshifters. He had been separated from them days ago and had been hiding in this cave, waiting for them. Finn steps to the edge of the mountain ledge and releases a series of thunderous roars that reverberate through the night. A distant roar answers. *"They're coming, Blue,"* Finn assures him.

Lyra asks Blue if he's hungry, but he insists he wants his family first. Lyra wraps her tail around Blue, holding him close. Within minutes, two massive shapes appear descending from the clouds. They approach with a swift dive, then level off just before landing. A large male dragon, pure black with equally black eyes, lands and exhales smoke, assuming an aggressive stance. Beside him, a giant female dragon with azure eyes, presumably Blue's mother, lands gracefully. She scans the area and soon finds her child next to Lyra. Blue emits a small roar and rushes to his mother, who envelops him in her wing, her nose and eyes checking him with concern.

Finn steps closer to the black dragon, whose posture remains cautious but slightly more relaxed. Lyra and Finn telepathically communicate with the dragon family about what happened and how we found Blue. The black dragon introduces himself as Drakkur, leader of the last small band of dragons in this realm. Azure, his mate, expresses her gratitude for our assistance. Drakkur requests to speak with me.

Lyra shifts and continues to mediate between the dragons and me. I stand before Drakkur, who gasps and approaches me, sniffing the air around me. Finn moves closer to me for support. I extend my hand and touch Drakkur's snout. *"It cannot be. Who are you?"* Drakkur asks, astonished. Azure's gaze is equally intense.

"I am Anwen Elwen of House Elwen of Eldoria," I say, my voice steady despite the turmoil within. "I am estranged from my father and House now, as I refuse to be dictated to about my mate and the destruction of dragons. I have come to understand that our realm and the Council of Elders have waged war on your kind, and I do not condone this."

Drakkur turns to Azure, then back to me. *"We knew and loved your mother,"* he says. *"She fought valiantly for the dragons; she was our friend."* The weight of his words hits me, and I collapse to my knees, allowing my grief to overtake me. My mother was slain defending dragons. Drakkur, Azure, and little Blue surround me, lowering their heads in a gesture of comfort. I reach out, holding them close, finding solace in their presence. Lyra adds, *"They are honored to have found a daughter of 'The Dragon Rider' and welcome you."*

For the first time, I feel a profound sense of purpose: to protect and defend dragons. Lyra conveys this sentiment to the other dragons. They have named me after my mother, "The Dragon Rider." Looking up at the dragons surrounding me, I declare, "I am honored to be your Dragon Rider. Before I can set things right for dragons, I must assist my mate in the human realm." Lyra reassures me, *"They understand and will continue to conceal their kind until your return."*

As Finn and Drakkur step away, Blue nudges me gently. I stroke his snout and say, "You are a brave dragon, Blue." He lifts his head and exhales a plume of cold air. Lyra translates his unspoken question, *"He wants to know when you will come back."*

"As soon as I can, Blue," I promise. "Take care of your family. I need strong, brave dragons to fight alongside me." Blue moves close, meeting my gaze. He telepathically communicates, *"I will be waiting for you."* I smile at him, "Look at you, already mind speaking. You are truly unique, Blue. I will return soon, I swear." Blue nods and rejoins his parents.

The dragon family then moves toward the cliff's edge, spreading their wings and launching into the sky, disappearing into the clouds.

TWENTY ONE

Challenge Accepted

I can't believe I've connected with dragons who knew my mother—dragons she fought beside! My emotions swirl inside me: pride, awe, disbelief. It's like something has clicked into place in my heart and mind, filling a void I didn't even know was there. I never knew her, but now... I feel stronger and more complete, carrying this piece of her with me.

Finn's voice breaks through my thoughts. *"I spoke with Drakkur. He understands our need to access the portal and travel to the human realm. He's willing to create a distraction, hopefully buying us enough time to activate the runes and open the portal."*

I nod, feeling the weight of responsibility settle on my shoulders. *"That could work... But I don't want them hurt, Finn. There are so few dragons left in this realm."* My voice is laced with concern, protective instincts flaring.

"Drakkur is a warrior," Finn reassures me, his calm presence grounding me. *"He can handle this with little risk to himself or their kind. I'll share the plan with you."*

I exhale, trying to release the tension in my chest. *"When do we go?"*

"At dark tonight."

"Good," I reply. *"The sooner, the better. Let me charge the runes with what's left of the sunlight."*

I retrieve the runes from their leather pouch, laying them out in the last rays of the sun. As I watch the fading light charge the stones, I think about what's ahead—traveling through the night by dragon flight, soaring through the clouds toward Rome. We're already a day late. Anxiety prickles at me; without warriors by my side, the mission feels more precarious. But there's no turning back now.

Maynard returns from her scouting trip, landing silently beside me. She describes what she's seen: about ten warriors surrounding the portal area, rotating shifts of five at a time, switching every twelve hours. She heard some of them bragging about sneaking in naps around two a.m., their weakest point.

"They're vulnerable around two," she concludes. The plan begins to take shape in my mind.

With our strategy in place, we rest while we can. The night deepens, and I gather the charged runes, packing them back into the pouch at my belt. I shift into dragon form, and together, we take to the sky, heading for the portal. We land quietly about a hundred yards from the entrance, concealed by the trees and shadows. I crouch low, watching, waiting... but there's no movement. No guards in sight.

A voice behind me startles me. "Hi, Anwen. It's safe for you to use the portal now."

I spin around, and there he is—a large man with dark brown shoulder-length hair, black eyes, and a muscular build. His smile is warm, and I can't help but grin back.

"I'm impressed, Drakkur. Thank you," I say, genuine gratitude in my voice.

"No problem," he replies, the smile never leaving his face. "Go get your mate."

Impulsively, I wrap him in a big hug, catching him off guard. His eyes widen, and Finn's laughter echoes in the quiet night. Together, we walk to the portal, and I place the runes in the stone, still feeling Drakkur's warmth as he disappears into the woods.

"Where did they put the guards?" I ask, curiosity piqued.

Finn chuckles, his dragon's voice rich with amusement. *"Well... the dragons were hungry."*

My eyebrows shoot up in surprise. I start laughing and boop his nose, saying, *"You know, some girls have cats, some have dogs...I have a dragon that breathes fire and shapeshifts and gets nose boops."*

Finn laughingly says, *"Yes, I can set entire armies ablaze, but we both know my biggest weakness is your nose boops."*

Still smiling, I turn my attention to focusing on the incantation. The next moment, we're pulled through the portal, back into the human realm.

I quickly gather the runes, checking on my team. Everyone's good to go. Finn shifts into his dragon form, and I climb onto his back. With a powerful leap, he takes off into the night sky, heading for the clouds. The darkness surrounds us, and I lose track of time, of place—only the vast sky and the distant destination ahead.

Our plan is simple: fly as long as possible, find secluded spots to rest, eat, and fly again. We follow this pattern for two days and nights, the journey stretching on. By the third day, I'm eager for news from Maynard, wondering if we're anywhere near Rome.

After cleansing in a nearby stream, I return to our camp, refreshed. Finn grazes nearby, his belly full of fresh grass. I pack the runes away, feeling their weight on my belt once more. Maynard arrives soon after, perching with the grace of a seasoned scout.

"We're about a half-day's flight from Rome," she informs me.

"Did you see Ashton? Or any of his men?" I ask, heart skipping a beat at the thought of seeing him again.

"No," she replies. *"I haven't had much time to scout the town yet."*

As the sun sets, anticipation builds inside me. I mount Finn's back, and we take to the skies once more. The thought of seeing Ashton again fills me with excitement as if it's been years instead of days. I let myself doze off, slipping into dreams of him—his half-smiles, his fingers teasing my ears, his touch sending shivers down my spine. I dream of running my fingers through his hair, feeling his warmth beside me.

I wake with a start as Finn begins to descend rapidly, dropping out of the clouds toward a cluster of trees. My breath catches as I spot the sprawling city of Rome ahead.

Down below, Ashton leans against a building, scouting a papal tower. A hawk's screech cuts through the air, and his head snaps up. Could it be…? He watches the hawk circle above him, recognition dawning. Quickly, he saddles his mount and follows the hawk's path, riding toward one of the city exits. His eyes never leave the sky.

And then, he sees her. He sees me.

I circle above him before flying toward the outcropping of trees down the road. He gallops after me, slowing as he enters the canopy, searching, listening. He stops, the silence thick around him.

"I've missed you, Dark Hair," I call out softly from the shadows. He turns, his eyes locking on me as I sit perched in the tree.

He dismounts, and before I can even catch my breath, I'm in his arms. I grab him tightly, our lips crashing together in a kiss that feels like coming home. His hands are everywhere—my hair, my face, my body—desperate to touch, to feel, to make up for the time we've lost.

Finally, we pull back, breathing heavily, our foreheads resting against each other. I inhale his scent, and he plays with my hair, and my ear, whispering how much he's missed his little mate.

We walk together toward the small camp. Finn, now in horse form, grazes nearby. He lifts his head and gives a small whinny in greeting to Ashton, who smiles and says, "Good to see you too, Finn."

Maynard lands on Ashton's shoulder, rubbing her head affectionately against his cheek. I gasp in surprise.

"She's never done that with anyone but me," I say, incredulous.

Ashton chuckles, a knowing glint in his eye. "She's female. She knows a good man when she sees one."

Maynard turns to me, her voice teasing. *"Oh, please. I'm just glad to see him taking care of my friend."* She lifts off, flying away, and I can't help but laugh. Having him here, with my friends, it feels... right. Complete.

Ashton's eyes scan the shadows, searching for any sign of the warriors before they land on me. I catch his gaze and offer a small smile. "I know," I say softly, "it's a long story. Sit with me by the fire, and I'll tell you everything."

The crackling firelight dances between us as I unravel the web of lies, treachery, and wonder that weaves through the past days. Meeting the dragons, discovering their connection to my mother, and their help with the portal—it feels like a dream. As I speak, Ashton's expression shifts from concern to quiet understanding. When I finish, he silently lifts me into his arms, settling me onto his lap. His warmth surrounds me, grounding me in the here and now.

"I'm sorry I wasn't there, Anwen," he murmurs, his voice rough with regret. I rest my head on his broad shoulder, feeling the steady rhythm of his heartbeat beneath my hand. "I've realized that when you're not with me, I shut down. I just... exist," I admit, my voice barely a whisper.

Ashton's sigh rumbles through his chest. "I understand. I've had to do the same on countless missions—shutting down and pushing emotions aside. But I never imagined my mate would have to experience that, too. I can't say I like it."

His head dips closer, and I feel his lips graze my ear, the gentle teasing of his tongue sending shivers down my spine. "I want to protect you from everything, Anwen," he whispers. "It weighs on me that I can't always be there. Maybe I'll just lock you away in my castle, keep you heavy with our children, and love you until you can think of nothing but me."

His hand finds my breast, his fingers teasing, circling, and pinching. A soft laugh escapes my lips. "Alright, lock me up, then."

He pauses, then laughs, pulling me tighter against him. "Don't tempt me, little one," he growls playfully, his deep voice sending a thrill through me. Gods, how I love him. With him, I can let go and feel carefree—just be his mate, not the warrior weighed down by duty.

Ashton fills me in on the latest plans. "We'll need to adjust a few things now," he says thoughtfully, "but I'm confident we can still defeat the Pope."

"I hope so," I reply, the weight of our mission pressing down on me. We have only a few hours until daylight, and we both know we need rest. But sleep, it seems, is not in the cards.

Ashton is spooned against me, and I can feel exactly how pleased he is to have me close. Mischief flares in me, and I wiggle my hips against him. His sharp intake of breath is followed by a quick slap to my bottom. I freeze, then flip over to face him, wide-eyed. "What the hell was that for?"

A wicked smile curves his lips. "You're teasing me, Anwen, and it's taking every ounce of control I have not to ravish you right here. That little 'tap' is just a reminder to behave."

I narrow my eyes at him. "Oh, so I shouldn't tease you at all?"

He chuckles, his voice low and dangerous. "You misunderstand. Love taps have different meanings at different times. Trust me, little one, there will come a time when you'll beg for them."

My face flushes at his words, and I huff. "You're making that up. There's no way I'd ever enjoy that."

His grin only widens. "We'll see," he whispers. "But for now, rest."

Despite my racing thoughts, sleep creeps in, and soon, I am drifting into his arms.

I awake to the softest brush of lips against mine. Blinking, I find Ashton gazing down at me, worry etched into his handsome features. My hand reaches up to touch his hair, then his cheek. He looks so troubled.

"I'm struggling, Anwen," he confesses, his voice a quiet rasp. "Watching you head into battle... it's aging me with worry. How can I ask you to stand aside when you are my equal in battle, but every part of me aches at the thought of losing you?"

I smile, though it doesn't quite reach my eyes. "Remember, Ashton, close off those emotions. Fight for our future. That's what I'm going to do."

He rests his forehead against mine, exhaling slowly as if trying to let go of the weight. Then, with a soft grunt, he rises to his feet and offers me his hand. We break our fast in silence, the looming battle ahead casting a shadow over us. With one last glance at each other, we mount our horses and ride toward the chaos wrought by the Pope and France's King.

TWENTY TWO

The Reckoning

Ashton leads the way into Rome, riding his warhorse with a commanding presence. I follow Finn, glamoring my ears beneath the hood of my cloak. Our capes drape over our armor, hoods pulled low to conceal our faces. Ashton navigates through the city, carefully noting landmarks, his eyes sharp and vigilant. I catch sight of the papal tower, and memories of my imprisonment and torture flood my mind. I force myself to push them down, refusing to give in to the fear clawing at my chest. Ashton rides back to me, concern etched on his face, and asks if I'm okay. I nod, though my body betrays me, breaking out in a cold sweat. Every instinct screams to escape this place, but I hold firm.

We finally arrive at the inn where Ashton and the Queen's spy are staying. After securing a stall for Finn, we cross the road and step into the inn's warmth. I choose a table against the wall, positioning us to watch the one entrance. Ashton orders our meal and joins me, his presence grounding me as the tension from earlier slowly ebbs away. I manage a tentative smile, and he responds by squeezing my hand. The tavern maid arrives with two large tankards of ale, making sure her ample bosom is as close to Ashton's face as possible. She leans in and asks, "Do you need anything else?"

Ashton, unfazed, sits back and raises my hand to his lips, kissing it without sparing her a glance. I stare at her and say, "We have everything we need. Just bring the food." She scurries off, and I turn to Ashton with a wry smile. "Do I have to fight off every wench who wants you? Because I will if I have to."

He chuckles and says, "No need. I ignore them, but they can be persistent." Our food arrives, and we eat in silence, both of us keeping a watchful eye on the inn's patrons. Once finished, I follow Ashton upstairs to his room.

Ashton closes the door and brings a finger to his lips. I wait, and after a few minutes, there's a series of coded knocks on the door. Ashton opens it, and a man steps inside. Ashton shuts the door and introduces him as Thomas, the Queen's spy. Thomas reaches for my hand and raises it to his lips, but Ashton growls and steps forward. Thomas sighs, dropping my hand, and looks at Ashton. "Have you fully mated her yet? Because you're acting like you have. How can you fight with your mate in the thick of battle when you can't even stand her receiving a peck on the hand?"

Ashton runs his hand through his hair, clearly agitated. "I honestly don't know."

I step in, my voice firm. "Thomas, don't question my mate's abilities. I don't. Don't mistake his love for weakness in battle. We are fierce and deadly, especially when we fight together. Now, what's your purpose here today?"

Thomas looks at me, his expression softening. "My apologies. I meant no offense. This mission requires precision and coordination. I didn't see any additional warriors?"

I explain, "You're correct. My father tried to stop me from coming, using our warriors and archers against me. I had to kill my own men to get here." Thomas stares at me for a moment, then nods. We sit at a small round table, discussing how we'll adjust our plans.

After agreeing on the revised strategy, Thomas excuses himself to meet with the leader of the Knights Templar and update him. Ashton also needs to see his men and inform them of the changes. I agree to wait in the room for his return. Once Ashton leaves, I share the plan with Finn and Maynard. Lyra and I also discuss our timing for the upcoming shift.

When Ashton returns, we continue talking late into the night, going over every detail and searching for any potential issues. At one point, Ashton looks at me, his eyes soft. "Do you know how it made me feel watching you set Thomas straight about our fighting together?"

I shake my head, and he says, "Loved, Anwen."

I reach out, touching his face, and press a gentle kiss to his lips. We're both somber, thinking of the battle ahead. Ashton whispers, "I was forged for war, but it's the thought of losing you that truly terrifies me." I hold him close, and as we start to drift off to sleep, I say, "I understand, but together, we are the storm that no evil can withstand."

The next night, just before midnight, we prepare for the mission. Dressed in all black, including masks, we check on the horses and make sure the runes are hidden. We meet Thomas in an underground tunnel leading to the papal quarters. The tunnel is dark and damp, with rats scurrying out of our way as we move through it.

We reach a gate in the wall and time the guards' rounds, waiting for the right moment. When the coast is clear, we remove the grate, slip into the hallway, and split up. Every guard we encounter is swiftly taken down and hidden. We eventually meet at the papal door, where Thomas picks the lock. We enter the room, but the Pope is nowhere to be found.

Thomas seems uncertain, his intel not matching up. Right on cue, a loud explosion echoes from the courtyard, throwing everything into chaos. We glance out the window and see guards scrambling in all directions. The Templars and Ashton's warriors are cutting through them, but beyond the papal gates, my heart sinks. A battalion of the Pope's soldiers is in military formation in the open area facing the papal building.

Thomas and Ashton argue about whether we should continue fighting or retreat. I step in, my voice steady. "We stand our ground. We use this building as our cover. Our mission isn't over until the Pope is dead. We'll find the mole later." I open the window and call down to the Templars and warriors, summoning them to join us outside the Pope's chambers.

The Templars and warriors arrive quickly, their faces pale from what they've witnessed outside the gates. Ashton and I step forward, and I watch as he raises his hand, his voice steady and calm despite the chaos. "We can still win this battle," he says. "We need a small group to head to the dungeons and free all the prisoners. If any can fight, give them weapons. We can't fight them head-on; we have to break their lines and attack from all sides."

I nod in agreement, even though the tension in the air is suffocating. The Knight Templar leader, Brian, turns to us and says, "We excel in breaking enemy lines. My men will gather and prepare. What will be the signal to attack?"

Ashton's voice cuts through the murmurs, strong and confident. "A dragon roar."

Silence falls over the group. All eyes turn to him, wide with shock and disbelief. I step forward to ease their worries. "We have dragon friends who will help us win this fight. Don't be afraid. A dragon will be in position behind the soldiers. When you hear the roar, attack from the front."

The Templar leader crosses himself, then turns to his men. "This is a holy sign of divine intervention. Our savior has given us the means to stop this unholy tyrant from killing our people. Templars and warriors, meet me in the courtyard."

As they hurry away, Brian glances back at us. "Do not let me down. The dragon had better be fighting for us." With that, he turns and follows his men.

I reach out to Finn through our connection. *"Now, my old friend, hurry."*

His response is swift. *"On my way already, Anwen. Lyra told me about the soldiers."*

I turn to Ashton, but he looks troubled. "Have you seen Thomas?"

I scan the area quickly, but Thomas is nowhere to be found. A sinking feeling settles in my gut. "No. I don't like this."

Ashton nods, his jaw clenched. "It's suspicious, but Thomas has always come through for me."

He steps closer, his hand on my shoulder, concern etched in his eyes. "Be careful. Lyra, watch after my mate." He kisses me quickly, then turns and runs down the hall toward the courtyard.

I take a deep breath, refocusing on the task ahead. Speaking through our bond, I contact Maynard. *"I'm coming out the west exit. Make sure it's clear of soldiers, and scout the best way for me to get behind the enemy without being seen."*

Maynard responds swiftly. *"I'm here. Your exit is clear. I'm scouting now."*

With Ashbringer in hand, I rush through the halls of the papal building. Maynard's updates guide me, and soon, I'm crouching in the brush, hidden from sight. Suddenly, her voice comes through urgently. *"Stop!"*

I drop to the ground, holding my breath. Ahead of me, two soldiers appear, talking in low voices as they relieve themselves. One grumbled, "I don't understand why we need so many men to capture or kill a small group of heretics."

The other soldier mutters, "They're not telling us everything."

As they finish and move away, Maynard gives me the all-clear, and I continue on my path, heart pounding in my chest. Finally, I make it behind enemy lines.

"Lyra," I whisper. *"Shift."*

I feel the power ripple through our bond as Lyra transforms, taking flight. Her roar echoes through the night, shaking the earth beneath me. I hear the fear in the soldiers' voices as they turn toward the sound. Chaos erupts around me—explosions, smoke, and shouts fill the air as the papal gates fly open. The Templars are in formation, galloping toward the front line with their weapons ready, their charge a thunderous assault on the enemy.

Ashton's warriors flank the sides, cutting through the chaos and confusion. I watch from a distance as the Pope's soldiers falter, their ranks crumbling beneath the relentless attacks. Above, Lyra soars, calling down rain to blind them, making the ground treacherous and muddy. She scans for the leaders of the Pope's soldiers, striking them down one by one with bolts of lightning.

I feel a surge of pride as I watch her protect Ashton, always vigilant. The battle is turning in our favor—until suddenly, I feel her pain. A searing heat course through our bond, and I know something has gone terribly wrong.

Lyra lands heavily in a nearby field, her wings damaged. I tell her, *"Shift,"* and look down at my arms, bleeding from deep wounds. "Thank the gods, it missed my arteries." I start tearing strips from my cloak to bandage my wounds.

As I tie off the last bandage, I hear a male voice behind me. "Time to go, Anwen."

I spin around, but it's too late. A blow to the back of my head sends me crashing to the ground. My world goes dark as rough hands lift me, and I'm thrown over a shoulder, carried away on horseback.

Through the haze of pain, I cling to one thought: Ashton. I have to get back to him.

On the battlefield, Ashton searches the sky for Lyra, but she's gone from his sight. Brian and his templar warriors have decimated most of the Pope's forces, but a new wave of soldiers charges toward them. French soldier reinforcements that shouldn't have been here.

Ashton and Brian regroup their men, forming a defensive circle. Archers are placed in the center, and shields are raised as the first wave of reinforcements crashes into them. Half their men fall; Ashton and Brian look at each other and realize they will not survive this battle. But they don't give up. Bloodied and exhausted, they stand their ground. The second wave hits and Brian goes down on one knee from a deep sword wound to his shoulder. Ashton's sword stops the next killing blow aimed at Brian and fights desperately, his strength waning, as he fends off another attacker.

And then, from above, a mighty roar splits the sky. The Dragon Lords have arrived. Finn leads them, flanked by two other dragons, their wings casting shadows over the battlefield. Ashton watches in awe as they descend, their fiery breath engulfing the enemy soldiers, their power unmatched.

The dragons tear through the Pope's reinforcements, flames turning night into day. The enemy is no match for their might, and soon, the battle is over. Ashton helps Brian to his feet, then turns to face Finn, who lands before him. The dragon's massive eyes meet Ashton's.

"I don't know where she is, Finn," Ashton says, his voice heavy with worry.

Finn roars in frustration, then kneels, offering his leg. Ashton turns to Brian, and the Templar leader says, "I will take care of the men and find the Pope." They grasp hands, and Brian says, "If you ever need the Knight Templars, we will heed your call, my friend."

With a final glance at the battlefield, Ashton climbs onto Finn's back. The dragon unfurls his wings, and with a powerful leap, they take to the sky. The other Dragon Lords follow, their eyes scanning the land below, searching for me.

I can only hope they find me in time.

TWENTY THREE

The Gathering

Maynard follows Thomas, her keen eyes tracking his every move. Finn asks for her location, and she replies, "Thomas is heading toward a castle near the Spanish Road. I'll let you know when he stops." Finn acknowledges her, and I hear him relay the information to the Dragon Lords. Drakkur's voice comes through, steady and reassuring. "We will find her, Finn."

As I lie unconscious in this unknown place, Ashton's fear for me surges through our bond, a wave of desperation that nearly overwhelms me even in my hazy state. He doesn't know where I am or who's taken me, but I feel his unrelenting determination. We survived that battle, not by luck but by sheer will and the dragons' support. I know he's proud of me, but his fear lingers like a shadow. He's aged years in a matter of days, and I know it's because of me. The thought of me fighting beside him—it terrifies him. There will be serious discussions about that when I'm back in his arms.

Through our bond, I sense Maynard nearing Finn and the others. She circles above, then swoops down toward Finn. Ashton lifts his arm, and she lands gracefully, pressing her head against his neck. I hear her relay my location to him, and he strokes her feathers gently, whispering, "I'm so worried for Anwen."

Before long, a castle looms into view, and Maynard screeches, taking flight toward it. Finn and the other dragons begin their descent, gliding down toward the towers. Drakkur shifts into his human form and joins Ashton on one of the towers, both of them scanning the castle for an entrance.

Ashton finds a door, but it's locked. He doesn't hesitate—he hacks the lock off and charges down the steps. Drakkur uses his dragon senses, sniffing the air and scanning the darkness. "I've got her scent," he says, his voice low. "And there's a man with her."

I feel Ashton's rage through our bond. His muscles coiled with tension, ready to explode. "He's mine to kill," he growls, his voice deep and dangerous.

Drakkur looks at him, concern flickering in his eyes. "I understand, Ashton, but you might need to calm down a little."

But it's too late. Ashton's already leaping down the final steps into the main chamber of the castle, his eyes locking onto me. I'm tied to a chair, my head slumped against my chest. Thomas stands beside me, a sword pointed at my neck.

Ashton roars, his fury shaking the room. Thomas smirks, not the least bit intimidated. "Well, well," he says, his voice dripping with disdain. "This mating thing really messes with you, doesn't it? One more step, and I'll take her head off."

I can feel Ashton fighting to keep control, forcing himself to stop and breathe. His eyes stay fixed on me, searching for any sign of life. "You're dead, Thomas," he snarls.

Thomas laughs, his eyes gleaming with madness. "All these years, I've served our Queen faithfully, and what has it gotten me? Nothing. When I found out your mate was a dragon shifter, I knew I had to have her. With her power, anything is possible."

"You've lost your mind," Ashton growls. "You can't control her."

"Oh, but I can," Thomas says, his grin widening. "If she bears my child, she'll do whatever I say."

Ashton's fury reaches a boiling point. "There's only one man she'll ever mate with, and it's not you."

With that, a dagger slips from Ashton's sleeve into his palm. In one fluid motion, he hurls it straight at Thomas, striking him between the eyes. Thomas's expression turns to shock as he crumples to the ground, dead before he hits the floor.

Drakkur whistles softly. "Remind me never to piss you off."

Ashton rushes to me, his hands trembling as he gently pushes my head back, brushing my hair from my face. His fingers search for injuries, finding a large lump on the back of my head, still bleeding. He unties me quickly, his hands moving over my body, checking and rechecking for any other wounds.

Drakkur touches his arm, but Ashton spins around, ready to attack. Drakkur raises his hands in surrender. "Easy now. Let's get her home."

Ashton takes a deep breath, nods, and scoops me into his arms. He carries me back up to the tower, his eyes never leaving me. When we reach Finn, Ashton's voice is steady but strained. "We leave now for my castle."

Finn nods, and Ashton carefully climbs onto his back, Drakkur lifting me up to him. As soon as I'm secure, Finn takes off into the sky, the Dragon Lords close behind.

When I finally awaken, a pounding headache greets me, and I groan softly. I blink and look around. I'm in Ashton's bed-chamber, and once again, he's asleep in a chair beside the bed, snoring softly. I close my eyes against the pain, then open them again to see him watching me, his eyes filled with worry. He looks exhausted, with a few more lines around his eyes and mouth, but he's here. He's mine.

He kisses my forehead, then sits on the bed, holding my hand tightly. He exhales a long, shaky breath and rests his head on my chest, silent. When he finally lifts his head, I see tear tracks on his face.

I reach up, wiping away the tears, and offer him a small smile. "I once thought strength was my greatest weapon until I realized it was your heart."

"I can't lose you, little one. Every time you raise your sword, my heart trembles- not because I doubt your strength, but because I can't imagine a world without you in it", he whispers, his voice breaking. "I'll follow you anywhere, even into the afterlife. The fear... it's like nothing I've ever felt before."

I stroke his cheek gently. "I'm tougher than I look. You know that."

He gives me a wry smile. "I do. But where you're concerned, I'm not. Look at me—I'm getting grey hairs over this."

I laugh softly. "Don't blame me for those grey hairs. That's just you getting old."

A knock at the door interrupts us, and Ashton calls for them to enter. The healer steps inside with a poultice in hand. "How are you feeling, Anwen?" she asks kindly.

"My head feels like it's about to come off," I admit.

The healer smiles gently. "I've got something that should help with that."

As she applies the poultice, Ashton's demeanor shifts. His body stiffens, and without a word, he stands. "I'll be back soon," he says, his voice distant, before leaving the room.

I frown, sensing something is troubling him deeply. Whatever it is, it will have to wait. The poultice starts to ease my headache, and I drift off into a peaceful sleep.

When I wake again, Ashton is back, carrying a tray of food. He sets it on my lap and sits beside me, his eyes full of affection. He begins feeding me pieces of fruit, a playful smile on his face.

"I can feed myself, you know," I say, amused.

He grins and licks his lips. "I know, but I like feeding you. I like watching you eat."

I roll my eyes, laughing. "You're so weird."

"Maybe," he replies, chuckling softly. He doesn't let me feed myself, though, insisting on serving me every bite. By the time I finish, my belly is full, and I feel much better.

I lean back against the pillows, looking at him. "Tell me what happened with the battle."

Ashton removes the tray and lies beside me, pulling me into his arms. He explains how close they came to losing—how the reinforcements arrived too soon and how the Dragon Lords saved them when all hope seemed lost. I listen intently, my heart racing at how close we came to disaster.

"It was that close?" I whisper.

He nods, his voice low. "Yes. The Templar leader and I thought it was the end for us, but we kept fighting."

I pull him closer, understanding his fear more deeply now. The thought of losing him terrifies me just as much. This fear of losing each other... it's overwhelming.

Ashton's voice softens as he continues. "I kept looking for Lyra, but I couldn't find her in the chaos. When the battle ended, I knew you were gone, but I didn't know where or who had taken you."

"Maynard," I say softly.

He smiles, his eyes brightening. "She has a special place in my heart now. She led us right to you. I owe her more than I can say."

"That's my girl," I whisper, pride swelling in my chest.

He glosses over the details of finding me and killing Thomas, and I don't push for more. It clearly bothers him, and I can see the toll it's taken on him.

Ashton changes the subject, his curiosity piqued. "How did you and Finn manage to bring the Dragon Lords to our realm?"

I smile, leaning closer. "Magic."

He starts teasing me, licking my ear and tracing my lips with his fingers. "Tell me, little one, or I'll make you want me so badly, and then stop."

I burst out laughing. "Oh, so that's how it's going to be? Don't forget—I can do the same to you."

He grins. "Touché."

I explain how Finn and I discovered that the magic runes originated with the Dragon Lords of Eldoria. When the wars between the elves and dragons began, and the dragons were losing, they entrusted the runes to an elf woman shifter, who was instructed to travel to another realm to keep them safe.

Ashton's eyes widen. "My mother?"

I nod, confirming his suspicion. "Yes. All dragons and elves with dragon genetics can use the runes to travel through time and to other realms. Your mother was from Eldoria and protected the runes here. She taught you how to use them, maybe hoping you'd return to the Dragon Lords of Eldoria one day."

Ashton is stunned, and the pieces of his life with his mother are finally falling into place. I continued, telling him about our discussions with Drakkur and how Finn had arranged for the dragons to help us. I explained that my mother had dragon genetics, that she was a dragon rider, and that she was likely killed for it. I told him about my father's betrayal and the steps I had to take to return here.

"Ashton," I say softly, "I have to go back to my realm. The dragons need to be free from the Council of Elders. They deserve to live in peace and thrive."

He nods, his gaze steady. "In this world of chaos and bloodshed, your love is the one thing that's pure. Where you go, I go."

We spend the night talking, touching, holding each other, reaffirming our love. By morning, Ashton helps me walk through the castle grounds. I visit Finn for some snuffles and hugs and make sure to give Maynard plenty of love, too.

Love for each other—this is what life is about.

TWENTY FOUR

So You Want to Play with Fire

As I smile to myself, a sense of peace washes over me. The battle and chaos have subsided, and for now, I just want to enjoy the tranquility of this moment. I decide to go for a swim and head toward the little secluded pond hidden among the trees. The air is cool, but the sun filters through the canopy, warming my skin. I slip out of my dress and chemise, letting them fall in a heap on the ground. Naked, I wade slowly into the water, feeling the chill envelop me as I move deeper.

Ashton hasn't been far from me lately, watching over me like I might break at any moment. His protectiveness is endearing, but I crave the feeling of freedom, even if just for a few minutes.

Unbeknownst to me, Ashton has followed. I sense his presence before I see him, standing just beyond the tree line, half-hidden in the shadows. Even when he thinks he's being subtle, I can always feel his eyes on me. The thought makes me smile, knowing he's watching, admiring.

I dive into the water, letting the coolness wash over me. Floating on my back, I feel the sun warming my breasts as they break the surface, my nipples rising to greet the sky. I know he's watching, and it stirs something in me—a desire to tease, to draw him closer. I flip over, stick my butt in the air, and dive underwater again, repeating the motion a few more times, knowing it's driving him mad.

Ashton, my ever-vigilant mate, finally loses his control. I hear a splash and feel the water ripple as he surfaces beside me, his hands finding my waist before I can react. He moves my hand away from where it had been teasing my own body, his voice low and rough as he murmurs, "Let me pleasure you, my mate."

I laugh, a soft, teasing sound. "It's about time."

His eyes narrow, but there's a spark of amusement in them. "You enjoy torturing me, don't you? Haven't I warned you about teasing me?"

I grin, remembering our earlier conversations. "I believe we've had this talk before. And my response was—blah, blah, blah."

His half-smile tells me I've hit a nerve. Before I can say more, he dives underwater. I lose sight of him for a moment, the anticipation building as I search the surface. Then, I feel his hands on my buttocks, lifting me out of the water. I gasp as he raises me higher, positioning me so that my sex is level with his mouth. He delves in without hesitation, his tongue finding its target, and I let out a sharp intake of breath. The sensation of his tongue working against me is exquisite—he licks at me, up and down, sucking and teasing with an intensity that sends shivers through my entire body. My hands tangle in his hair, holding him closer as I chase the feeling building inside me.

But just as I'm on the edge of release, Ashton stops. He lowers me back into the water, and I'm left panting, the pleasure so close yet just out of reach.

I glare at him, frustration coursing through me, but he only laughs. "I warned you not to tease."

Two can play this game, I think. Reaching down, I wrap my hand around his shaft, moving slowly, deliberately, watching as his control begins to slip. His head falls back, and a deep groan escapes him as I work him to a fever pitch. His hips move against my hand, and just when I know he's on the brink, I stop.

He snaps his head forward, his eyes dark, and for a moment, I think I see them flash red. But before I can say anything, his mouth is on mine, devouring, demanding, his tongue mimicking the rhythm he promises with his body. I grab his hair, pulling him closer, letting myself get lost in the taste of him, in the fire he ignites in me.

Ashton's control is slipping. I can feel it in the way he grips me, the way his voice growls with need. "Do you want me inside you, my mate? Will you share yourself with me in every way possible?"

I nod, breathless. "Yes. I want you to love me, to please me in every way possible."

His growl reverberates through me as he pulls me closer, his hands kneading my buttocks as he rubs me up and down his shaft. His fingers find my labia, teasing, opening me to the water's cool embrace as he moves me. Then, one of his fingers slides behind me, circling before pressing gently into my backside. I gasp at the unexpected sensation, but his lips are on my neck, whispering for me to relax, to let him pleasure me.

He moves his finger slowly, in and out, adding another between my folds, stroking both entrances in a rhythm that's driving me wild. His other arm holds me steady as he continues sliding me along his shaft, and I can feel my climax building again. "Don't you dare stop," I warn him.

His smile is wicked against my skin, but he keeps going, playing me like a finely tuned instrument. The pleasure crests and I feel myself shatter, wave after wave of ecstasy washing over me. He doesn't stop until I'm limp against him, my body spent and trembling.

I rest my head on his shoulder, breathing heavily. "Wow," I manage to say.

He chuckles, nibbling at my ear, bringing me back to him. After a few moments, I turn my head and bite his neck, holding on to the thick muscle with my teeth. His growl is low and dangerous, and before I know it, he's positioning me, his shaft at my entrance. With one swift, hard movement, he's inside me, filling me completely. I barely feel any pain, just the overwhelming sensation of being connected to him, of him filling every part of me.

He moves slowly at first, his hands gripping my hips as he thrusts deeper. My body adjusts to him, and soon, we find a rhythm, his hips slapping against mine in time with my movements. Every thrust sends another wave of pleasure through me, and I grip him tighter, wanting more, needing more.

It doesn't take long before he's on the edge, his growl turning into a loud shout as he reaches his release. I release his neck and lick the spot where I bit him, smiling at the satisfaction on his face.

"Wow, little one," he says, laughing softly.

He carries me out of the water, laying me on our clothes on the pond bank. We stretch out beside each other, the sun warming our skin, the birds singing in the trees, the scent of blooming flowers surrounding us.

"That was amazing," I say, "but don't let it go to your head."

He turns his head, grinning. "Well, my head can get bigger to please you."

I laugh and roll over on top of him. He wraps his arms around me, drawing circles on my back as we share our thoughts and fears. Our connection, both physical and emotional, feels stronger than ever—sealed in every possible way.

I straddle him, sitting atop his growing erection, rubbing myself against him. He raises me slightly, guiding himself to my entrance, and we move together again, this time slower, savoring every sensation. Just as I'm about to reach my climax, he pulls out and flips me onto my stomach, covering my back with his body, his erection pressing between my buttocks.

I try to push against him, wanting control, but he slaps my buttock lightly, his voice a commanding growl. "I'm in control, Anwen. Not you. I decide when you peak. Do you understand?"

The dominance in his voice sends a shiver through me, and I find myself liking it. "Yes," I breathe.

He rubs his hand over my buttock, soothing the sting of the slap. "Good girl. Now, don't think—just feel."

He raises himself off me, pulling my hips up so I'm on my knees, my shoulders down. His shaft slides along my seam, lubricating us both as he describes in that deep, gravelly voice all the things he wants to do with my body. His words alone are enough to make me burn with need.

Then, with a strong, steady thrust, he's inside me again, deeper this time. He picks up the pace, his hips slapping against my buttocks as he grips my hair, pulling my head back toward him. His breath is hot against my ear as he whispers how mad with lust and love I make him.

I'm close, so close, but just as I'm about to reach the peak, he slows, kissing my back, smoothing his hands over my buttocks. I start to push against him, desperate for release, but he slaps my buttock again, reminding me, "I control the pace and when you come. Trust me, Anwen, when you peak, it will be intense."

His voice is both a promise and a challenge, and I surrender to it, letting him take control. His thrusts pick up again, his fingers teasing my entrance as he moves, and then he slides his thumb into my backside. The sensation is overwhelming, a mix of pleasure and pressure that makes me moan.

"That's it, purr for me, little one," he growls, increasing the pace, his thumb and hips working in perfect tandem.

Finally, he commands, "Now, come, Anwen," and I erupt, the pleasure so intense it feels like fire coursing through my veins. I cry out his name as waves of ecstasy crash over me, one after another. My body convulses uncontrollably beneath him, every nerve alive with the overwhelming sensation. Ashton doesn't stop, driving me higher, deeper into the pleasure, until I feel like I'm being consumed by it. His hips slam against me with a fierce intensity, and then I hear it—a deep, guttural growl that signals his own release.

He pulls me back against him, holding me tightly as his own climax overtakes him, his body shuddering with the force of it. I feel him twitch inside me, his release filling me as he lets out a long, satisfied groan. His hands grip my hips to steady me as his thrusts slow, finally stopping. He lowers me gently to the ground, both of us panting and spent.

As we collapse onto the grass, he keeps me close, his body still pressed against mine. He licks my ear again, sending a pleasant shiver down my spine, and I smile, feeling utterly content. When he finally lifts himself off me, he rolls to his side, propping himself up on one elbow to look at me.

Ashton's eyes are soft, filled with warmth and love. "I can't wait to show you more," he whispers, a playful grin on his lips.

I turn my head to look at him, still catching my breath, and smile back. "Neither can I."

We lay there for a while, soaking in the peacefulness of the moment, the world around us seemingly holding its breath. The sun is warm on our skin, and the sound of the water lapping at the shore is a soothing melody in the background. For the first time in what feels like forever, everything is quiet. Safe.

TWENTY FIVE

Coming Home

The message arrives early in the morning, carried by a swift messenger. Ashton reads it silently, his face hardening as the news sinks in. The Knights Templar have captured the Pope and the Inquisitor. Justice was swift and brutal—both were presented to the families of their victims, those who had suffered under their cruelty. Beaten beyond recognition, they were finally burned at the stake. The letter mentions King Philip VI, who has gone into hiding, moving from his residence at The Conciergerie Palace to multiple other residences, surrounded by guards. The religious artifacts and money taken during the conflict are now safely locked away, though the Templars remind Ashton that the favor he owes them will be called upon one day.

When Ashton tells me about the message, I can see the relief in his eyes, but I know there's more on his mind. His loyalty to England still pulls at him, and before we leave this realm, there are duties to be fulfilled. He's summoned to a private meeting with Queen Elizabeth at Windsor Palace. The gravity of the battle and the betrayal of

Thomas weigh heavily on him, and I know the Queen will want to hear it all.

He meets with her, explaining in detail the events that unfolded—how Thomas, once loyal, turned against him, driven by greed and delusion. He tells her of Father Gabriel Thorne, the man who spurred the Pope into investigating me for witchcraft and Ashton for heresy. The Queen is composed as always, though I can imagine the surprise hidden behind her calm exterior. She compensates Ashton generously, but when he mentions Thomas, her displeasure is clear. Father Thorne will be "dealt with," she says, leaving little to the imagination. Before their meeting ends, Ashton informs her that we will be leaving soon, though our return is uncertain. She insists that another private audience be arranged when we do come back.

It takes months for us to prepare to leave this realm, months of planning, and ensuring that everything is in place before we pass through the portal. Banoff has proven more than capable, stepping up to manage Ashton's holdings and warriors. The men who fought by our side in battle are rewarded handsomely. For the families of those who fell, Ashton ensures that their losses are honored with compensation.

Banoff and Ashton work out a system—a way for Banoff to reach him should anything go wrong. A simple sign left at the portal entrance will be enough to signal Ashton, though neither of us knows when we'll return. There's another journey ahead of us now, an adventure waiting in Eldoria.

The day arrives, and with a mixture of excitement and bittersweet farewells, we head to the forest portal. The familiar energy of the portal pulls us through, and as soon as we arrive in Eldoria, Maynard takes to the skies, scouting ahead for any sign of danger. Finn quickly alerts

Drakkur, who invites us to their lair. It's only a few hours' journey, but as we approach, the sight of the mountain lair fills me with warmth.

The Dragon Lords greet us with open arms, their human forms gathered around the massive cavern. The mountain is more intricate than I remember, a maze of tunnels leading to the heart of their home. The light filters through the cavern roof, creating a warm, almost ethereal glow. There's fresh water from an underground stream, and the smell of roasting meat fills the air, welcoming us to a feast already prepared.

I spot Blue running toward me, his little face lighting up as I crouch down to scoop him into my arms. I swing him around, both of us laughing and when I set him down, I can't help but smile. "I've missed you, Blue," I say, ruffling his hair.

He grins, then grows serious. "I've been practicing, you know. My flying and my fighting—so I can help you fight one day."

I glance at Drakkur, and he nods. "He's determined," Drakkur says with a hint of pride. "He wants to fight by your side one day."

Blue hugs my leg and dashes off to join the other children, and I can't help but feel a swell of affection for the young dragon.

Drakkur calls the Dragon Lords to gather, and they form a circle around us. The air is thick with anticipation, their powerful presence filling the cavern as they stand tall, their scales gleaming under the natural light. Drakkur's deep, commanding voice echoes through the space as he addresses them. "Dragons of Eldoria," he begins, "we gather today to welcome a new member into our noble family. Anwen, the Dragon Rider, whose strength and wisdom will guide us in the battles to come."

I step forward, feeling the weight of their eyes on me, but there's warmth here—respect. "My fellow dragons," I say, my voice steady but laced with humility, "It is with great honor that I accept this role among you. Together, we will uphold our traditions and ensure that our kingdom prospers for generations."

The dragons bow their heads in reverence, and I feel the connection between us grow stronger. Ashton watches from the shadows, leaning against the cavern wall, his hands in his pockets, a proud smile on his lips. I can feel the intensity of his gaze, and I know we'll need to have a conversation about the future battles ahead. I see the worry in his eyes, the fear of losing me again. He'll fight for me as fiercely as he fights with me, but this is a conversation for another time.

A mighty roar of approval shakes the cavern as the dragons pledge their loyalty. The sun dips lower, casting long shadows through the openings in the roof, but at this moment, we are united. A new era has begun in the heart of Eldoria, led by the strength of the Dragon Lords and their Dragon Rider.

Later, as the feast winds down, Ashton and I are shown to our quarters. Finn heads off to rest, and Maynard finds a high perch to roost. I settle into the room, the weight of the promises I've made sinking in. "That was a lot of responsibility I just accepted," I admit, leaning into Ashton's embrace. "I hope I can help them reclaim what's rightfully theirs."

He tightens his arms around me, his lips brushing against my hair. "We'll help this realm find balance again, Anwen. Between the elves and the dragons. This is our realm, too." He kisses me lightly, giving me that half smile that always makes my heart skip.

In one swift motion, he scoops me up, and I instinctively wrap my legs around his waist. His grin widens as he carries me toward the bed. "Now," he says in a low, playful voice, "let's continue your mating education, shall we?"

I laugh softly, already feeling the heat rise between us. "Yes, please."

Acknowledgment

To my family:

- My sister, Marci, my brother, Bill, and my nieces, Lilly and Amber have supported me with encouragement and feedback throughout this book-writing journey. Without your unwavering support, I'd probably still be staring at a blank page, wondering if I could somehow train the dog to type.

To my friends:

- Brian, thank you for your friendship and support. I greatly value our friendship. I could not have done this wonderful celebration without your help. I believe you *are* a Knight Templar. Seriously, who knew launching a book was like planning a royal wedding?

- Dawn and Mike, thank you for your gracious offers for the voiceovers for the audiobook, I can't wait to see what you both can create! Thank you for your generosity and support (and for being such awesome gaming teammates!). Your voices will forever echo in my head, and not just from our epic gaming sessions.

To all the Westhoff's Warriors book group:

All of you are the best friends I could ever have asked for. Thank you so much for supporting this journey with your kind words and feedback. Also, thanks for pretending to enjoy and not fall asleep during my endless discussions about writing a book.

To the editors, marketing, and advertising teams:

Thank you for helping me fine-tune this first book, "Chronicles of a Timebound Warrior," and the support and technical skill shared were so valuable. You turned my chaos into a coherent story, which is nothing short of a miracle.

To my wiener dog, Shoo Boo:

The best doggie partner for providing unconditional love, despite me becoming one with my laptop. Your judgmental stares during my writing marathons kept me grounded.

To my readers:

I hope you enjoyed this journey with Anwen and Ashton to different worlds and realms. And remember, if you don't like it, please send your complaints to Shoo Boo—he's the real boss around here!

Fly by my website for exclusive book updates, epic character art, and maybe a dragon-sized surprise or two at https://lynnwesthoff.com/. Help a dragon out – please leave a review on Amazon, or risk being fire-roasted (but in the nicest way possible)!

Teaser

"To those who hear whispers on the wind, may your mind's eye always see beyond the horizon. Watch closely, for in the shadows, vampires stir, wizards and witches weave their spells, and the hum of mechanical dragons fills the air— more awaits in the next tale."